SONY LABOU TANSI was born in Zaire in 1947. He taught English at the Collège Tchicaya in Pointe Noire before joining the Ministry of Cooperation in Brazzaville. He then moved to the Ministry of Culture. His first novel, *La vie et demie* (1979), was awarded the special jury's prize at the First International Festival of *Francophone* held in Nice. He has published plays and several novels, and directs a theatre troupe in Brazzaville. He also writes poetry.

CLIVE WAKE was born in Cape Town. He studied at Cape Town University and at the Sorbonne. He taught at the University of Rhodesia (now Zimbabwe) and at the University of Kent at Canterbury, and is now Emeritus Professor of Modern French and African Literature. He is the author of criticism, editions and translations in the fields of modern African and French literature.

SONY LABOU TANSI

THE SEVEN SOLITUDES OF LORSA LOPEZ

Translated from the French by
Clive Wake

Heinemann

Heinemann Educational Publishers
A Division of Heinemann Publishers (Oxford) Ltd
Halley Court, Jordan Hill, Oxford OX2 8EJ

Heinemann: A Division of Reed Publishing (USA) Inc.
361 Hanover Street, Portsmouth, NH 03801–3912, USA

Heinemann Educational Books (Nigeria) Ltd
PMB 5205, Ibadan
Heinemann Educational Boleswa
PO Box 10103, Village Post Office, Gaborone, Botswana

FLORENCE   PRAGUE   PARIS   MADRID
ATHENS   CHICAGO   MELBOURNE   JOHANNESBURG
AUCKLAND   SINGAPORE   TOKYO   SAO PAULO

Les Sept Solitudes de Lorsa Lopez © Editions du Seuil, 1985
Translation © Clive Wake, 1995

Les Sept Solitudes de Lorsa Lopez first published by Editions du Seuil in 1985
This edition first published by Heinemann Educational Publishers in 1995

British Library Cataloguing in Publication Data
A catalogue record for this book is available from the British Library.

ISBN 0435 905945

Cover design by Touchpaper
Cover illustration by Graham Baker Smith

Phototypeset by CentraCet Limited, Cambridge
Printed and bound in Great Britain
by Cox & Wyman Ltd, Reading, Berkshire

95   96   97   98   11   10   9   8   7   6   5   4   3   2   1

To all those who helped me
to come into the world:
My father,
My mother, my grandmother,
Alphonse Mboudou-Nesa,
Arlette, Pierrette
Henri Lopes, S. Bemba . . .
And may women now fight
with weapons other than
those of the female woman

That which you think defenceless is defended by the shadows.

Victor Hugo

Woman is the very place of birth.

Edouard Maunick

Africa has always been thought of as the civilization of the word. I have observed the exact opposite: we are in fact the civilization of silence. A mulatto silence.

S.L.T.

Foreword

Art is the strength to make reality say what it would not have been able to say by itself or, at least, what it might too easily have left unsaid. In this book, I argue that there should be another centre of the world, that there should be other reasons for naming things, other ways of breathing ... because to be a poet nowadays is to want to ensure, with all one's strength, with all one's body and with all one's soul, that, in the face of guns, in the face of money (which in its turn becomes a gun), and above all in the face of received wisdom (upon which we poets have the authority to piss), no aspect of human reality is swept into the silence of history. I am here to speak on behalf of that part of history that has not eaten for four hundred years. My writing will be shouted rather than simply written down, my life itself will consist of groans and screams and being pushed around, and never being allowed simply to live. I am going in search of man, who was once my brother; in search of the world and of things, who were also once my brothers.

S.L.T.

1

Estina Benta

On the eve of the disastrous Thursday when we were to learn that Lorsa Lopez was going to kill his wife, on the eve also of the fateful day when Valancia was to celebrate its second phoney centenary, at five o'clock in the morning, at the very moment when the muezzin of the mosque at Baltayonsa called the faithful to prayer, when Fr Bona of the Sacristy crossed the bayou on his way to Elmano Zola's butcher's shop, we heard the earth cry out from the direction of the lake: a long succession of groans and mournful rumbles, a kind of convulsive gurgling from inside the rocks, to which even the sea seemed momentarily to listen. We, the people of the Coast, called this strange phenomenon the 'cliff's cry'. The Nsanga-Nordans referred to it as the 'cliff's laugh', but that only demonstrated their crass stupidity.

'Just six thousand one hundred and thirty days more and it'll all be over,' said Fartamio Andra do Nguélo Ndalo.

The cry had lasted three minutes but everyone, from Valtano to Nsanga-Norda, had heard it, and they all said it was because of the orgies of the Coast people that the cliff had taken to preaching. To singing, almost.

Misfortunes never come singly. We hadn't sold our pineapples that year, because our President had insulted America at the Sixteenth Paris Conference on the price of raw materials. Out of revenge, the Americans refused to eat our pineapples, and the French had supported them by refusing to eat them out of modesty, the Belgians because they understood, the Russians out of timidity, the Germans out of simple bloody-mindedness, the South Africans by intuition, the Japanese out of honour ... Anyway, for one reason or another, the whole world refused to eat our pineapples. Instead of giving in, the authorities passed a law requiring overseas residents to eat impossible quantities

1

of pineapples, morning, noon and night: that is, three kilos per head per day! 'Serves them right,' everyone said.

The foreigners all began to hate us: us, our country and our laws. 'It's those perch-eaters of the Coast who dreamt that one up,' they maintained. 'The Nsanga-Nordans have more sense.' Then the cliff started all that groaning and dreadful screeching, all that inexplicable yapping. That call to silence.

It was the same cry we'd heard at the same hour of the day years before, when the authorities had decided, for the seventh time, to move the capital from Valancia to Nsanga-Norda: 'We can't stay here, this place belongs to the devil,' they said. And so, for several long months, walls, bridges, municipal gardens, town squares, swimming pools, railway stations, all went on their travels, by air and by water, by rail and by road. Even the water from the artificial lake of the Village of Passions, the seven drawbridges, the thirty-nine mausoleums, the fifteen triumphal arches, the nine Towers of Babel, the sixteen stars of Nsanga-Norda, as well as the twelve mosques from the period of our Holy Patron John Valance, were all transported to the new capital. Not forgetting the Gold Boulevard, the three billion or so bones from the cemetery of Harma Hozorinte, the solid-gold street lamps of the former District of the Eleven, the seventy-nine thousand artificial trees from Marsien Park, where it was said a prehistoric man had been found in a granite sarcophagus. The find had been kept in Westina Museum, but a group of sailors had stolen it and then set sail from off the Island of Solitudes. 'So much for the Greco-Latin lie,' everyone said.

The place where the sarcophagus was found is now known as the 'rectangle of death', where human beings are reduced to heaps of bronze. The first person to be reduced to a heap of bronze was Lucio Attinelio, the brother of Estina Bronzario. May he rest in peace!

Also taken away were the seven thousand modillions, the nine hundred and fifteen monoliths, obelisks and arches, as well as the head of Christ carved out of what remained of the Island of Eldouranta, which had been devoured overnight by the angry sea. In fact, the original head had been carried off by the subjects of King Joani in 1497. The Portuguese had left us a basalt outcrop, out of which they had hurriedly carved a mulatto Christ, with a pot belly and fat cheeks, who turned his back on the sea. The real one had looked out towards the Island of Solitudes, with his right side turned towards the Coast.

'The Coast has been cursed because of that loss,' explained Fartamio Andra do Nguélo Ndalo.

'What coming and going!' sighed Estina Bronzario. 'They're not even going to leave us any food.'

'There's nothing we can do about it,' Fartamio Andra advised. 'But they'll be back, like before. Nsanga-Norda isn't the sort of place to keep a capital.'

The government notary who was supervising the decapitalisation announced that nothing would be taken from the Bayou quarter, where the tombs of the Founders Line of Valancia were, nor from Baltayonsa, the former university, closed for committing high treason. 'It smells terrible there.' All the corpses had a white band tied around their foreheads bearing this inscription, written in Indian ink: 'Don't shoot! We stand for solidarity.' (Three thousand and forty-four white bands were found when, a week later, Estina Bronzario unexpectedly decided to defy the authorities' ban by burying the bodies.)

The government notary went to see Estina Bronzario wearing a humourless smile, which he had prepared far too long in advance, and which revealed his three teeth of ugliness. 'I've been instructed to tell you, Madame, that you will continue in office as mayor of our new capital. Allow me to congratulate you with all my heart and all my . . .'

'Get out!' Estina Bronzario retorted. 'I'm not your dustbin. I was born in honour and in honour I shall die.'

When the notary persisted, she spat into his government face a mixture of tobacco, anise and pimento. (Estina Bronzario chewed pimento instead of kola because, she said, it preserved a woman's inner youth.)

At the time, Estina Bronzario had enough spunk to stand up to any sort of male, but when the news that she'd spat on the notary reached the ears of the authorities, she was placed at the disposition of her balls. She lost her salary, and was banned from setting foot in Nsanga-Norda. For insulting the flag, said the statement announcing the decision, published in the official newspaper and available on request. 'They're not going to shut me up like this!' laughed Estina Bronzario.

3

At noon, and then again in the evening, on the eve of the day when Lorsa Lopez was to kill his wife, the earth gave three more small cries from the direction of Nsanga-Norda, two from the direction of the ocean, and one small cry from the direction of Valtano, before lapsing into a silence that terrified us. We waited on tenterhooks for it to end, as if it were some kind of game. Fartamio Andra do Nguélo Ndalo claimed that the earth always cried out in Valancia to mark important events. It had cried out when the papal nuncio, Estanzio Bienta, was assassinated. It had cried out when the monster, Yogo Lobotolo Yambi, was born of father unknown to the madwoman, Larmani Yongo.

The monster had seven heads crowned with a brass crest, twelve arms of unequal length, one leg in the shape of a grooved column ending in a sort of elephant's foot, thirteen highly polished jagged tusks, with thirteen orifices, four of them shaped like trunks ending in what resembled umbrellas made of solid limestone and which snapped like slow-worms when you touched them. It was said that these four orifices served as eyes, nostrils and ears. A long pipe-like rod, also made from limestone, and situated at the root of its forked leg, served as its penis, at least that was the opinion of Lorsa Manuel Yeba, the monster's maternal uncle: sexual organ and waste hole. Whenever the baby cried, the Coast people put their hands over their ears. Because of our complaints, his mother had tried to drown him in the estuary, down by the Bay of Lotes, but, each time, Yogo Lobotolo Yambi had walked back through Valancia howling his infernal howl and regained the maternal home, with the heavy iron bar that was supposed to keep him at the bottom of the sea still around his neck. In spite of the widespread protests, and in spite of the position adopted by the authorities, who thought that a monster like that could easily seize power and hold it for centuries (and who proposed that he should be thrown into the pit of fire at Porto Indiano or into the rectangle of death), Fr Bona of the Sacristy, in the just name of Jesus, brought up the child until he reached the age of sixteen, when he left the shadow of the Lord and the five a.m. mass and dived into the sea at Afonso Bay, leaving behind him footprints six feet in diameter which sank to a depth of between five and twenty inches, depending on the soil. The monster had left some scratches on the walls of what remained of the cathedral, where Fr Bona said mass. Some said it was a message. They were strange drawings, figures of glyptodonts and giant flexographs, and what looked like whelks. Depending on whether they were from Valancia or Nsanga-Norda, Mahometans or Christians, deists or atheists, glyptographers suggested a number of meanings for the graffiti. To the Christians, who shared the view of the glyptographer Ruano de Dios Louma, the message was simple and clear: 'Next time, the fire.' At the time, Yogo Lobotolo Yambi had grown to the obscene size of six Nsanga-Nordan elephants.

The very last time the cliff had cried out was seven years previously, on the unforgettable day when the rebels of the Sieda Merdaï had taken Elmuconi Zamba to Valancia and blown out those mangy-dog brains of his that had got the people of Valtano involved in the conspiracy that was holding up the decapitalisation. 'He asked for it,' sighed the authorities.

Fartamio Andra do Nguélo Ndalo couldn't understand why the earth hadn't cried out when the students had gone on strike, a few weeks before the arrival of the notary who was to organise the seventh decapitalisation; or why it hadn't marked the first decapitalisation war, which had brought the Founders Line into conflict with the Nsanga-Nordans forty years before. Nor could the poor woman understand why the earth had failed to cry out to mark the students' last stand when, after they'd been on hunger strike and refused to negotiate for eighty-two days, the authorities, moved to pity, asked the Seventh Infantry Battalion to travel the two hundred and twelve kilometres between Valancia and Valtano and shoot the poor buggers, whom death itself declined to kill.

Then nothing happened in Valancia for eleven months, neither great joy nor great mourning, neither coming nor going, nothing at all, until that disastrous morning, the eve of the Thursday when Lorsa Lopez was to kill her. While the indomitable Estina Bronzario and the women, out of pure and simple obstinacy, were busy organising the centenary banned by the authorities, the earth cried out.

'Sang, almost,' people said.

'As if from birth pains,' explained Fartamio Andra to the women, who were busy cooking the food for the banned centenary.

'I think Baltayonsa cried out more loudly than Jesus Island.'

'What are you up to, Estina Bronzario?' the mayor demanded to know, furious.

'Since there aren't any men left in this country, I'm setting the women to work,' replied Estina Bronzario.

They erected barricades across the road to the bayou and across the road that ran alongside the wood by the lake. They piled the shed built by Estina Bronzario's grandmother at the time of the last centenary high with liquor. They brought over the huge pots that had been simmering gently for the past two days, giving off their tantalising smells and offering glimpses of onion, garlic and vegetables from Nsanga-Norda swimming on the surface . . . Strings of sausages, heaps of barbecued lamb, mountains of grilled meat, basins of soup, bright-coloured sauces, *mandella* sauces, picket sauces, *lantanni* sauces, azanio sauces, nuts *Hélène*, laws of the Coast, fine monkey sands, ruptured livers, bronze milks, gigantic gâteaux the size of a fisherman's hut, *misalas* with herbs . . . The whole of the Bayou quarter was permeated with the smell of cooking and wine. An endless stream of hungry children presented themselves, declaring their hunger in the customary words: 'The nose wants to eat but the nose has no hands.' People licked their lips. Stomachs were ready.

In the Tourniquet quarter, other women were busy sewing party dresses and carnival costumes. Still others were practising the rumpus and the rumba, down by the railway station. Wearing her mother-of-pearl smile, Estina Bronzario bore her august bronze stature from the kitchens to the sewing rooms, an ageing but still beautiful princess, endowed with that beauty which takes a lot of cooking and which lifts the lid of age, beautiful in gesture and voice, the collapse of her features belied by the ultimate achievement of that perfect harmony which is a blend of strength of feeling and obstinacy of spirit. And every part of her body was a tender reminder of the time when she used to dance the Nsanga-Norda rumpus and enfold men in the many delights of her flesh. 'A woman full of vitamins, that Estina Bronzario,' people said of her.

All night, the women cooked and sewed, while the young girls knocked on doors distributing invitations. At two o'clock in the morning, the mayor, accompanied by the judge, Marcellio Douma, and the photographer, Nertez Coma, came to see Estina Bronzario again and begged her not to provoke the authorities.

'Our region has a bad enough reputation with them as it is, Estina Bronzario. Celebrate anything you like but, please, stop this centenary nonsense.'

'We're a proud people, we have our honour to uphold, Marcellio Douma. We have twenty-seven centuries of bearing trouble with dignity behind us. The Coast eats fish, Nsanga-Norda eats meat. Who doesn't know that?'

'Thanks to you there'll be more unnecessary bloodshed, Estina.'

'It's a question of honour, Marcellio Douma. Oh, I know you think I'm talking nonsense. But there's no cause higher than honour. It's the very meaning of life. We of the Coast think and live by our honour. Unlike the meat-eaters of Nsanga-Norda, who are fit only for eating and shitting.'

The judge asked Nertez Coma to photograph Estina Bronzario's excesses and then left in the company of the mayor. At four o'clock, the women decided to have just two hours' rest, so that they would be fresh and ready for the festivities prescribed by the hardest of the hard, Estina Bronzario. They'd scarcely laid their heads on their pillows when the earth began to cry out, and he'd set about killing her, as we all knew he would.

'He could've chosen some other day to kill his whore.'

'There are seven days in the week, and he had to choose our one!'

Lorsa Lopez killed his wife following an incident which everyone from Valtano to Nsanga-Norda thought utterly trivial. How could a man like Lorsa Lopez, the son of Lopez Dario and Dona Maniana Cuenso, do such a thing? High Commander of the Legion, former Minister of Finance, he was a man of the most exemplary honour who, like Estina Bronzario, had resigned because of the seventh decapitalisation, who'd stood up to the authorities and gone to Nsanga-Norda in spite of his ban: 'It's the land of my fathers, after all.' A man who was held in almost legendary esteem and veneration by the whole Coast. A man who, during the first forty-four years of his existence, had shown himself to be a model of good sense and moral balance. We couldn't understand it. We blamed this screwed-up century, this pointless century, this century of bullshit. We concluded that man was so afraid and so ashamed of man that he had become gutless and unpredictable, that all he could do was make a noise. We were living in the age of the carved atom and highly polished noise . . . What a disaster!

'He could have killed her some other day,' sighed Fartamio Andra.

'Yes, he could have,' echoed Fartamio Andra do Nguélo Ndalo. 'He killed her with all the spitefulness of a mulatto. Valancia is rotten. Poor Estina Benta. What could she have done to him? I saw them only yesterday evening down by the bayou, near the Tourniquet: they were kissing under the big Indian fig tree, like a couple of holy innocents. They greeted me, and I asked her to come and help with the cooking for the centenary when they had finished having their fun. She arrived at seven o'clock smelling of their bodies. I asked her to go and wash herself, she smelt like a pigsty. Then she prepared the gâteaux and the rice fritters; she cooked the *zambroglios*, and the aubergines in wine. As no one in Valancia can cook barbecued doe like her, I asked her to do that as well. She only left at four in the morning, with everyone else. What could she have done to him, for heaven's sake?'

All that bullshit among the petticoats! Valancia was changing. The wives of the most peaceable men were having it off with the first fly-parter that came along. No one on the Coast could understand it. The monumental corruption. The decline in morals, the collapse of all sense of honour. Women were opening their legs like you open your fingers to look at the sun. The young women were making three-quarters of their bodies accessible to all eyes, and since the eyes are the doors of vice . . . We blamed the whites: 'When the body has its fill, the spirit retreats.'

'Armensah Fandra went over to her, while she was preparing the barbecued doe, and whispered in her ear: "Don't go home, Estina Benta. Today's the day when he must kill you." And when Estina repeated aloud what she'd said, we all laughed, because, in spite of Nansa Mopata's gloomy prophecy, we thought she was too beautiful, poor Estina Benta, to be killed by a man.'

'How, God of all gods, could he kill that poor woman?'

In all the villages, in all the quarters of the town, at every corner of every street, people declared their surprise: how could he have done it? No one had ever killed anyone in Valancia. Even the authorities, who in our country have the right to kill, had only ever exercised this right on three small occasions of no importance whatsoever: with Elmuconi Zamba, with the strikers – who'd had to be killed because death had declined to kill them – and, finally, with Estanzio Bienta.

It was early one morning in July, when many stay in bed because it's chilly outside, and couples make the most of the warmth between their thighs and the smells of love left behind from the night. We heard screams from the direction of Lorsa Lopez's pigsty. We realised that he'd begun to kill her.

Because she was busy with the preparations for the centenary, Estina Bronzario wasn't to hear about it until after nine o'clock, when she'd already put on her mauve velvet crinoline to receive her guests. Fartamio Andra tried to hide what had happened from her: 'She'll brood over her friend's death and spoil the centenary.' But we're only human, and we can't hide our joys and our sorrows, our convictions and our hopes . . . Estina Bronzario came back from the bayou like a whirlwind, her throat swelling with rage, the white-hot metal of her eyes all bloodshot.

'How can you dance when she's lying under a sheet? I'm postponing the centenary. Lorsa Lopez's pigs can come and celebrate her murder and eat all this food.'

She overturned all the cooking pots, all the dishes of food, threw all the meats, soups and sauces into the street, and aimed a hefty kick at the bunch of gladioli Fartamio Andra was to present to Fartamio Andra do Nguélo Ndalo, the oldest woman in Valancia and the last of the Founders Line. She delivered another kick at the red tulips and peonies that Nertez Coma was to present to the oldest of the old men. She overturned the pots put ready for the noshing competition and the drums of agave juice intended for the boozing competition.

'How can we celebrate while she's lying under that sheet?' said Fartamio Andra. 'They've cut her up like a pig and given her to the flies.'

She crossed herself, and a big tear fell from each of her eyes. Fartamio Andra do Nguélo Ndalo also wept two tears of the same size. When her anger had subsided, Estina Bronzario called us into her room, where we'd never set foot before, Nelanda, Marthalla and I. She was sitting on her bed, crying bitterly. Her face was set hard, and her lower lip shook. 'Not satisfied with turning us into domestic animals, now they want to kill us.'

It was the first time we'd ever seen her weeping her word of honour. 'They can fuck the cow when they've killed me, not before.'

She produced a small pestle which we saw was made of pure gold. She placed three grotesque looking vegetables into the mortar, three Nsanga-Norda pimentos and three aubergines. She added a few drops of Valtano wine, tore three strips from her underclothing, and tied three knots, repeating in a quavering voice: 'They can fuck the cow when they've killed me.'

She told the three of us to come closer and spit into the mortar, three times, then to take the earth of our ancestors, throw it into the saliva and grind it all together while we murmured: 'Woman of honour, blood of the word.' Seized by a tremendous shudder, we began to dance the rumpus of the great of the Coast. My body felt light as air, as if I'd been freed from the pull of gravity. At the same time, I was filled with a feeling of absolute pleasure and peace. My heart melted inside my breast. I'd never before felt myself so true, so happy, so at one with everything. My senses were transported way beyond anything they'd ever experienced before. The light became like nothing I can describe. At the end of this ritual, Estina Bronzario took our hands in hers, all together, and spat into them a mixture of tears and mucus. She told us to rub the saliva into our navels, then to slap ourselves three times on the pussy and dance the rumpus of Nsanga-Norda, while she cried out: 'Three thousand eyes in the sky, three thousand eyes in the stones', and sang this song:

> Nge tata dzioka
> tala ba ngungulu
> bakwiza mu banda
> mpele ngidi fwa kwa
> ngwaku wambindamana
> meki ma ngungulu.

> Let us fly, father
> the monsters are coming
> let us die rather
> since your mother

10

wanted to eat the eggs
of a monster.

'Men have become leopards.'

'Yes, they have.'

With an artistry that can only come from the mouth, Fartamio Andra told the story of the murder, employing words only she could find, constantly varying the tone for, she said, the art of naming is above all the art of getting the tone right.

'Early in the morning, after the ventriloquies of muezzin Armano Yozua, we heard shouting. It was an animal sound that shattered our ears and ripped the air to pieces, the sound of a gorilla vibrating the vaults of the dawn. It must have been heard in Nsanga-Norda:

' "I'm going to pack you off to the devil with all your games. I'll send you to him without a face. With all your bullshit and your bitch's heart."

'The poor woman called for help, and we heard her voice, nearly drowned by her husband's bellowing, as in the days when she sang at the conservatoire: "Help me! He's killing me!"

'Doors and windows were opened, revealing shadowy figures crossing themselves.

' "I'm going to pack you off to the devil, and you can take those pig's guts of yours with you."

'The whole quarter could hear the blows. He hit her with his fists, his feet and his head, with the insistent rage of a wild beast. With a methodical rage. He struck every part of her broken body, while she screamed for help and the whole village crossed themselves: "Oh God, what is happening to that poor Estina Benta?"

' "Since the women of this town have started playing at being men, nothing's right any more. It's all the fault of the whites. They've mixed everything up: the roles of the puppet, the epileptic and the idiot. Their money has killed our soul. I'm going to pack you off to the devil for good."

'While she screamed for help, he went into the pigsty. He came back with a spade and struck her three true male blows, breaking the spade – so he gave her two more hefty blows with the handle. Then he went and fetched a pickaxe and began chopping her like wood. He split her

11

body open and, ripping out her smoking guts, he tore at them with his big wild animal's teeth and drank her blood, to appease the anger knotting his soul.

'"You filthy bitch! You're going to pay for what you did."

'He cut her up, slit open her thorax, hacked her bones, tore out her breasts, threw away her womb, and took out "your wickedness and everything you kept there to enable you to play such a lousy trick on me – on me, who loved you to distraction. This is how you thank me. Now you'll pay. You wanted to play cunt. You wanted to play the slut. I'll give you fucking slut."

'He went into the pigsty, wiping his forehead with his shirt, red with sparks of blood and flashes of meat.

'Came back with meat hooks, hung her right thigh on the palaver tree.

'With this fat, that grub, and those pieces of pork.

'"You wanted to play cunt. I'll give you bloody cunt, without a head or a tail."

'He fetched all the tools from his pigsty: meat hooks, picks, forks, felling axes, machetes . . . millstone. He finished off his crime with the pickaxe. One last blow, which was heard throughout the town. Until siesta time, the body lay in the town square, still calling out: "Help me! He's killing me!"

'Dismembered, disembowelled, completely covered in red clay, crawling with flies stuffing themselves on blood and gore, her body garlanded with her guts, she lay there, moaning. No one brought her the help she wanted. Her voice gradually faded away. "Help me! He's killing me!" From her bloodless vocal cords came a hard, metallic, grating sound. Until two in the morning. "Help me! . . ."'

We couldn't understand how the whole town could have turned its back on Lorsa Lopez's crime. On Friday morning, at the time when Armano Yozua called the faithful to prayer, Fr Bona of the Sacristy crossed the bayou and went to the town square. His Benedictine's cassock was wet with dew. 'Help me! He's killing me!' He saw the body and crossed himself several times. 'God! What a disaster!'

Other people from the quarter passed by and, like the priest, crossed themselves uneasily.

'Gentle Jesus, what's happened to her?'

12

'Her man's killed her.'

'What could she have done to him, the poor woman?'

'She gave him lice.'

'Lice?'

'Yes! Real Nsanga-Norda *lab** lice.'

After committing his crime, Lorsa Lopez left the spade, the pickaxe, the big butcher's knives, the fork (which had lost two of its prongs), the hooks and his leather jacket at the scene, and shut himself in his pigsty, with his forty-seven cycling pigs, his dog, his two cats, and his parrot, which endlessly repeated: 'She gave him *lab* lice.' It was whispered that the parrot had revealed the name of the lover who'd passed on the lice, but no one really knew who – Nertez Coma, or perhaps Salmano Ruenta. We also suspected the judge.

We all thought Lorsa Lopez was going to kill himself in his pigsty, out of shame; that his pigs – as voracious as killer whales – would eat his body, and that when the police arrived, all they would find would be the murderer's gnawed bones.

On Friday 7 July, the mayor came to see the body and asked Nertez Coma to photograph it.

'*Lab* lice, fair enough, but he could've killed her some other way,' said the judge.

The mayor admitted privately that he preferred this crime to Estina Bronzario's centenary. 'The authorities wouldn't have thanked us.'

'Did he have to kill her in such a dreadful way?' said Nertez Coma, indignantly.

On Saturday morning, the judge came and put a sheet over the body. He placed large stones at each end to hold the sheet down, because the wind swept continuously across the town square. We waited for the police to arrive. At the time of night when dew begins to form on objects left outside, and while Fartamio Andra's insomniac cocks crowed, we heard a cry from the town square: 'Help me! He's killed me!'

'It's Estina Benta's voice,' said Estina Bronzario. 'He obviously hasn't killed her completely.'

Four months after the event, the police arrived from Nsanga-Norda

* We say either *lap* or *lab*. We got the word *lab* from Lorsa Lopez's parrot.

13

in great state, with motor-cycle escort, brass band and all the rest. They drove along the Rouvièra Verda, crossed the Bayou quarter, arrived at the scene of the crime via the station, and stopped for a moment by the sheet, which was still held down by the stones put there by the judge. But they didn't carry out their investigation. The disappointed mayor laid out the enlargements of the photographs taken by Nertez Coma on the day of the crime. As they returned in the direction of Nsanga-Norda, they stopped in the Tourniquet quarter to gaze hungrily at Elmano Zola's twin daughters, who were swimming naked in the Rouvièra Verda and displaying the flaming orbs of their breasts for the benefit of anyone who cared to look at them.

'Aren't they delightful!'

And since the girls always liked to throw water over the men who watched them, the officers of the law took the trouble to investigate the twins' breasts and pussies. It was, in fact, because of their epilepsy that the twins swam naked in spite of their age. The whole of Valancia knew they were still virgins, as no one, however beautiful they might be – no, however provocative they might be – would have dared investigate their pussies for fear of catching Nsanga-Norda fever, which is what we call the type of epilepsy that makes you shake for hours on end and sends you running for miles with your tongue hanging out. The eleven gentlemen of the police jumped into the Rouvièra Verda in full battledress and bathed with the epileptics until nightfall, when ten of them had to leave because, according to malicious gossip, they'd brought a veterinary nurse with them instead of a qualified doctor. Others suggested that the police had forgotten to bring a surveyor's chain and rule from Nsanga-Norda. The real reason for the departure of the police wasn't even made known forty-seven years later when they returned to carry out the investigation, by which time very few of those who were old enough all those years ago to act as witnesses could remember very much about it. No, no one ever found out why the police came and then left without saying anything or collecting any evidence. At any rate, not before the revelations of Sergeant Elmunto Louma who, at the time of the crime, arrived with the beard of a forty-year-old and couldn't leave with the others because the beautiful breasts of Elmano Zola's younger twin had pierced his heart, in every sense.

14

'I'm staying to love you at my leisure.'

'Aren't you afraid of catching the Nsanga-Norda sickness?'

'What do I care if I live or die by your love? I'll be happy to be buried by your side in this earth which has given us everything.'

Theirs was an ardent love, untouched by Estina Bronzario's sex strike. But the younger twin flung herself in an epileptic fit from the top of the cliff, and the sea refused to return her body to us. In spite of a search lasting months, Elma Zola Dehondara had to make do with a cenotaph, just as Fr Bona and the Beauty of Beauties, Zarcanio Nala, were to do later. Elmunto Louma adopted the habit of drinking agave water at the bar which his mother-in-law had opened after giving up the butcher's shop, which no one dared patronise any more.

When he was completely drunk, he'd give vent to his anger. 'What a pathetic lot you are in this god-forsaken place! Thanks to you, I've lost my peace of mind and the woman I loved. You're in such a mess, you say it's the authorities' fault, but I know that Estina Benta's murder's a community crime that's just come to roost on all that bullshit of yours about lap lice. It lets you blame the federal police for kicking their heels. How can anyone kill his wife, his true wife, for anything so ludicrous as giving him lice? And when you think, for God's sake, how much that poor Lorsa Lopez loved his whore . . . And just look how the population has grown from three thousand tadpoles to four million souls in only a few years! Seven hundred thousand families of shit who've moved into this shambles under the crazy pretext of waiting for the police to return! If you think that a man like me, an Elmunto, son of Elmunto Zuka, who was fathered by Elmunto Zecakani, who was himself fathered by Elmunto Kunga, son of Elmuntara Kungu, son of Elmuntara Kunguna, the practical son of Elmunto Koca, who came from Yoltansa, not from Nsanga-Norda, a farmer of yams not aubergines, who never in all his life ate the flesh of the salamander, and Elmunto Carcassore was his father! . . .'

For hours on end, with his bottle of *sanctari* – which he liked to drink with lemon – in front of him, he raved on about his ancestors, as far back as the ninety-second generation on his father's side. Couldn't remember anything about his maternal ancestry. Emptying his bottle, he'd wind up: 'No, sisters! You're hiding an eel under all that lather of yours about lap lice. We Yoltansans aren't given to

15

sucking up to people. We live and die in the open. And I tell you, the only man the Coast has is a woman, Estina Bronzario. When she's killed, the Coast'll cease to exist.'

Seven months after the spectacular visit of the police, Lorsa Lopez came out of his pigsty. No one was surprised that there were no more pigs and no dog. Only the parrot, which kept repeating: 'Raw, he ate them raw.' Lorsa Lopez was as fat as the hippopotamuses of the Rouvièra Verda, and under his bushy beard hung a thick, streaky dewlap, full of folds and alive with jiggers.

'Apparently it was a community crime,' people were saying.

'What's a community crime, anyway?'

'Oh, a kind of holocaust.'

'No, sister. You must put yourself in poor Lorsa Lopez's place: he loved Estina to distraction. You'd see them kissing and fooling about like a couple of turtle-doves. Then, suddenly, it was all over! Her behaviour was a disgrace! We all knew here on the Coast that she'd given him Nsanga-Norda lice.'

'Lice, or was it the pox?'

'Genuine Nsanga-Norda lice, fat and voracious as only Nsanga-Norda lice can be. They suck all a man's blood and spunk.'

'How awful!'

As a sign of mourning, Lorsa Lopez stuck seven nails, which he called his 'solitudes', and a dozen needles into his dewlap. He put them there every morning, at the time when the crime had taken place, and removed them in the evening, just before the sun went down. We knew that Estancio Dizi had mourned his mother by throwing himself nine times from the roof-top, breaking his back four times, and that Nertez Coma had mourned his first wife for forty moons without seeing the sun once, hardly drinking, and eating only three aubergines a day – and what kind of aubergines? Aubergines from Nsanga-Norda, well known for their extreme smallness and bitterness. We also knew that Yongo Yozua had mourned Valtamio Fonsa for sixteen years and several months. But the longest and most austere mourning was that of Lorsa Lopez.

'Oh, God! She's dead. What'll become of me?' he wept, emerging from the pigsty as if he'd only been there for a few hours.

He wept before the strips of sheet, held down by the stones, that

16

covered the bones of the dead woman. During the siesta, he took the old machete, eaten by rust and insects, and chopped open his left foot to complete his mourning.

'What a disaster! What wickedness! How could they let me commit this crime?'

He bandaged his wound and limped to Nsanga-Norda, where, with his savings, he bought a round stone coffin with a thick moquette lining on the inside. He gathered up all the bones – down to the tiniest, smallest bits – and reassembled the skeleton. But, just as he was about to proceed to the burial, assisted by the children and the onlookers, the mayor and the judge arrived to tell him what we all knew.

'You can't bury her. We have to wait for the police.'

'What?' said Lorsa Lopez, in surprise. 'The police haven't been yet?'

'They've gone to fetch a surveyor's chain and a folding rule,' sighed the judge.

'What a mess this god-forsaken place is!' said Lorsa Lopez.

During the first six years following the abortive burial, we saw him limping about, bleeding from the needles and nails in his dewlap, blackened with charcoal and ashes, his head shaved like an egg, devoured by Baltayonsa fever and scabies. We saw him coming and going, singing the hymn of the Seven Solitudes, day and night.

Valancia had once again become a city because of the crowds that flocked there to wait for the police and the final outcome of Lorsa Lopez's crime. 'It's a strange story. We'll wait here, my family and I, to see how it ends.' The town abandoned by the seventh decapitalisation was reborn, grew and prospered with Estina Bronzario, the woman of bronze, the hardest of the hard, at the centre of its life.

At the time of the crime, Fr Bona of the Sacristy had been the only really white white in Valancia. Now we counted thousands: those who drilled for oil out in the estuary, those who excavated the origins of man in the chalk of Baltayonsa (and who claimed that man is descended from the ape, whereas our own legends say quite clearly that Yonko Yoanko Kongo and his wife, Fartamio Andra Doupès Lama, were descended from the beast with the long neck and lunar skin whose huge skeleton had been found in the chalk at Valtano by the seekers after skulls), those of the National Pineapple, and those who fished for sturgeon off Afonso, mostly Russians and Spaniards.

The French had exclusive rights over the gold mines and the phosphates of the Island of Solitudes, while the Americans hunted the atlantosaurus in the tidal reservoirs of Quenso-Norte. The Canadians contented themselves with trying to find an explanation for the cliff's cry and for the death of the millions of lote, chub and cycling crabs that had covered all the shores of the Coast three days after the Thursday when Lorsa Lopez killed Estina Benta. As for the Dutch and the Chinese, they tried to find an explanation for the death of thousands of good-luck humming-birds four weeks after the crime, and for the incredible noise emitted by a *malavond* tree that grew in the estuary forest: the tree had been cut down dozens of times, but it always grew again the next day and resumed the singing of its song, which we called 'the song of the devil' and which the Mahometans of Nsanga-Norda called 'the poem of the exiled', no one knew why.

Lorsa Lopez became our bad conscience. We'd looked on while he killed his whore. Now that he slept in the stone coffin he'd bought in Nsanga-Norda, and came and went barking and bellowing the hymn of the Seven Solitudes, as he called the song he sang day and night, we saw him as all of us, as if we'd all lent him our arms to commit his crime.

Armensah Fandra bitterly resented the fact that Estina Benta had met her attempt to warn her with insults because she was too beautiful to contemplate her own death. 'I shouldn't have given up. But I was afraid there'd be a scene. Put yourself in my place. She could've thought I envied her her man.'

One evening, Estina Bronzario summoned all the women she called her war council to her room: Fartamio Andra, Marthalla, Anna Maria, Nelanda, Sonia O. Almeida, Fartamio Andra do Nguélo Ndalo and me. One place was empty: Estina Benta's. In the empty place, Estina Bronzario had lit an enormous red candle with a dancing purple flame that seemed strangely motionless.

'Estina Benta's time has come,' she said.

Armano Yozua was calling the faithful to pre-dinner prayers. Estina Bronzario chewed a red pimento, licked her lips and smiled. She arranged her fichu, looked at her medals and reflected for a long time. Fartamio Andra smoked her pipe; she broke a piece of kola, ate it, and held out a red pimento to Estina Bronzario, who chewed the pimento in the same way as Fartamio Andra chewed her kola. It was the time of day when, at the moment of the crime, the voice of the dead woman was to be heard calling out in the garden: 'Help me! They've killed me.'

'If the police don't come within the next three weeks, I'm going to have Estina Benta buried,' said Estina Bronzario.

'Do you think that's wise?' asked Fartamio Andra.

'We've waited thirteen years after all,' said Sonia O. Almeida, our sister back from Brazil, who believed that God and hell were Brazilian.

'The police haven't been because it was only a woman who was killed,' said Estina Bronzario. 'They're welcome to treat us like monkeys or lagans, but not to kill us.'

'Let's wait a little longer,' said Anna Maria.

Estina Bronzario always listened to her. We felt that she evinced a certain weakness with regard to Anna Maria because the latter had never in her fifty years been a mother. And Estina Bronzario called her *madre*.

The fifteenth year following the crime, all Valancia, including the mayor and the judge, were convinced that the police would never return. It was therefore decided that the bones of the deceased woman would be buried at the place where she'd been killed. Reality and dreams can be negotiated. Truth, never. It always lays down inexorable conditions.

Fr Bona brought candles and gave the blessing. Valancians crossed themselves as they'd done on the day of the crime. The mayor provided beer, the judge a dozen sheets. Lorsa Manuel Yeba had seven diamonds placed on the coffin and made the arrangements for the funeral banquet. Estina Bronzario's women, as well as Estina Bronzario herself, were to do the cooking. The bones were washed, polished, then covered with a layer of Nsanga-Norda varnish. The plastic surgeon, Carlanza Yema, faithfully reconstructed the dead woman with Nsanga-Norda bird-lime mixed with sawdust from the ailanthus tree and pink chalk. In spite of the parrot's revelations, malicious gossip still had it that the lice had originally come from the mayor, since he was providing eighty cases of iron-water and twenty of fire-water for the festivities that were to follow the burial. In reality, the mayor's gesture was probably dictated by his everlasting desire to show how well he was doing, for want of being able to show anything else. No one had any confidence in him as mayor, for all he did was engage in pointless display paid for out of money sent by bearer cheque from Nsanga-Norda. His budget fell under four heads, as follows: entertainment, fourteen thousand francs; public health, sixteen thousand one hundred and twelve francs; street decorations and flags, thirty thousand seven hundred and fifteen francs; contingencies, one thousand two hundred francs. Since we no longer had a bank in Valancia at the time of the crime, the mayor used to send Nertez Coma to Nsanga-Norda to collect the town hall's funds. The mayor's salary, as we all knew, was sent to him every fortnight with the first person calling at N.anga-Norda.

'Are you going to Valancia, sir?'

'Yes, I am.'

'That's convenient. Could you please take the mayor his pay. Tell the judge and the photographer that we'll send theirs as soon as we can.'

But the judge and the mayor had found a way of making money by selling a stream of bits of paper on their own account. They also sold land, which according to the constitution then in force belonged to the people, that is to say, to the authorities. We all knew that the mayor could definitely not have given Estina Benta lice, nor indeed any other woman. We knew that as a result of a nasty pox passed on to him by the Abyssinian singer, Martinez Sayilassié, who'd come to Valancia before the seventh decapitalisation, the mayor and his wife Leonora Dosandoval had separated. All he had left in place of his procreative organ was a crust of oozing, peeling flesh. Such was the mayor: his heart in thrall to money and the fear of losing his job as mayor, his pisser confiscated by the Abyssinian, and his head gnawed by a large pair of ears that danced the rumpus and made Salmano Ruenta laugh. The judge, Marcellio Douma, had been given the somewhat unkind nickname of 'true copy of the mayor', because his ears, too, danced all by themselves.

The coffin lay open for a time in the part of the cathedral that Fr Bona and his flock had fiercely defended against the authorities at the time of the decapitalisation.

'You will have to move your diocese to Nsanga-Norda.'

'But, Mr Government Notary, Nsanga-Norda is a bastion of Mahometanism.'

'In that case, just move half of it.'

After fierce discussion, negotiation and argument, it was decided to hold the wake for the deceased woman at Estina Bronzario's house, so that we wouldn't have to mourn her at the home of her murderer. We shed tears as if she'd died that very day, and sang and danced the funeral rumpus all through the night. At the burial, Marcellio Douma read the prayer and the mayor the seven hundred telegrams sent to the authorities asking for the police to return. Then the photographer, Nertez Coma, read the forty-five requests for the deceased woman to be awarded the Order of Nsanga-Norda. Obviously, these appeals had got nowhere.

'Because Estina Benta was only a woman,' shouted Estina Bronzario.

There was a painful silence after Estina Bronzario's outburst. You could hear the flies buzzing and nostrils inhaling. None of the men dared speak; they all wanted to avoid exciting the women. There were so many of them that they could've ordered the men to leave and let them handle the burial on their own. We all knew that women didn't officiate at burials. Fartamio Andra proposed that the town square should be named after the deceased. This proposal gave rise to another wrangle. The men wanted it to be given the name the deceased woman bore at the time of her death.

'It's more correct!'

'You aren't going to name the poor square after a murderer of women!' said Anna Maria, indignantly.

Estina Benta wasn't the deceased woman's real name either. She'd acquired it at an official dancing competition in Nsanga-Norda, because throughout her performance the head of the authorities, waving his arms in the air, had kept calling out 'Benta Estina', which means 'flesh of dreams' or 'flesh of celebration'. She hated this name, which the populace had thereafter foisted on her in order to mock the authorities. And since the people don't know how to forget, the name had stuck.

'You surely aren't going to honour the bad faith of the Nsanga-Nordans?' ventured Lorsa Manuel Yeba, the murderer's younger brother.

But no one could remember the deceased's maiden name. Some thought it was Larmanta Fandra do Mboudou Nisa. Others said it was Larmantès Salvio. Yet others said it was Nersandio. In spite of the fact that its origin nauseated us, we named the square 'Estina Benta Square'.

'It's safer,' said the judge.

'It's safer,' acknowledged Estina Bronzario.

After the burial, the women marched from the scene of the crime to the deceased's bedroom. They laid their fichus on her bed and burnt Nsanga-Norda bird-lime and incense before dancing the rumpus of honour inside the room. Each of them placed a piece of her velvet crinoline on the bed. They donned the cloth with black and white squares, and painted their faces with kaolin and their lips with white powder from Nsanga-Norda. They all put on the crown of feathers of the grieving widow. Fartamio Andra set at sixteen moons the period during which they would not open their cloths to a man. Woe betide the fool who spurned the majority's decision! She'd either menstruate continuously or catch the Nsanga-Norda sickness. This women's talk made the men smile, but knowing that Estina Bronzario would always be Estina Bronzario, they accepted that they would have to steel themselves to endure this enforced abstinence.

'Lucky Salmano Ruenta who can fool his balls with a nanny goat or a pig,' muttered Elmano Zola, the butcher.

Lucky, too, Estando Douma of Nsanga-Norda, who'd made himself a do-it-yourself vagina out of bird-lime and seal foam, never having managed to meet the woman who could endure his feature-length bangs. 'He always needs two days of erotic rumpus to get that pond-snail's slime of his out,' people said. That's why women steered clear of him.

'Estando Douma's going to be a rich man,' commented Elmano Zola.

He was right, for within three months of the women's decision, Estando Douma had received nine hundred and thirteen thousand orders for his screwing machine; he'd taken on seven hundred and fifteen workers to chop down bird-lime trees and three hundred others to fish for seal foam in the tidal reservoirs at the entrance to Nsanga-Norda.

22

The other decision taken by Estina Bronzario's women was no less of a constraint for the men. In future, men would take their wives' names when they married in Valancia.

'They can give us lice, all the lice on earth,' the butcher muttered. 'They can give us the pox and all the mushrooms in the world, but not their names.'

It's not altogether certain how Elmano Zola's pronouncement reached the ears of the women. The next morning, on opening the deep freeze to get out Fr Bona's daily half-kilo of liver, which he came to collect just as Armano Yozua was finishing the morning call to prayer, Madame Elmano Zola, still too bleary-eyed to make out anything clearly, was confronted by the most horrifying sight: three pieces of husband with a strip of vellum stuck between his teeth. On it, the following words were written with a cosmetic pencil and underlined with nail varnish, as we all saw later when we came to have a look, our faces streaming with hot tears: 'Women are also men.'

'Valancia is rotten,' said Fr Bona, crossing himself. 'The people here are thirsty for death.'

'What shall we do, Father?' asked the widow, overcome with horror.

Her voice dried up. Her hands trembled like the mayor's ears, her big eyes wept in silent suffering, her face was drawn like the strings of a guitar, her forehead was covered in sweat, and her bosom danced stupidly under her mauve dressing gown.

'How can we love death?' muttered the priest.

Pinching it between her thumb and her index and middle fingers, the widow blew her nose noisily, directing the jet of snot through the window. For a long time, the priest gazed at the pieces of husband, unsure whether or not he should bless them. Mesmerised by the monstrous sight of human flesh mixed up with cow's flesh, he couldn't decide how many times he should cross himself in order to secure God's mercy. Such depth of human crudity sent him reeling, as if the meat, the blood, and the strong odour of flesh had made him drunk. And the silence! The haughty silence of slaughtered flesh. And above all, the rather silly smile on the corpse's lips, at once mean and sublime. The priest crossed himself three last times, then a sound like a creaking weather-vane came from his throat: 'Call the police, but first give me seven days' supply of calf's liver.'

While the widow pushed aside the pieces of husband to get at the calf's liver, which she had difficulty in distinguishing from her husband's in the overfull freezer, the priest opened his prayer book, mumbled the *Magnificat* and blessed the freezer.

The widow set down the meat without being really sure whether it was calf or human: three and a half kilos for six thousand three hundred francs. Her hands trembled in spite of her effort to control them. The scales also trembled; it was almost as if they, too, wanted to cross themselves.

'What makes us behave so shamefully?' the priest grumbled, shutting his prayer book to pack his seven days' supply of dubious calf's liver.

We should perhaps mention that years later, many years later, when the police finally came to carry out their investigation, the police surgeon, Artanso Paolo Nola, wondered how Elmano Zola could have lived his forty-two years with a cow's liver.

'How can we build with shit?' asked Fr Bona, picking up his wicker basket.

He left the butcher's shop and walked straight ahead until he reached Valmazo's shop, where he bought seven Nsanga-Norda tomatoes and set off again. Everyone was surprised that he didn't take the rue de Nguélo to the Tourniquet quarter. This itinerary brought him to the mission between six o'clock and seven-forty. We were surprised, too, that he didn't have his prayer book open in his right hand and his wicker basket, the work and gift of our brother Loumoni Yambi, in his left hand. Everyone knew what the wicker basket contained at that time of day: half a kilo of calf's liver, seven heads of celery, seven tomatoes and three Nsanga-Norda pimentos. Usually, the priest made his first crossing of the bayou upriver from the railway station and reached his destination by the Nsanga-Norda road, while continuing to read his prayer book, as his eyes no longer needed to watch a route his legs knew by heart.

The priest didn't stop at the stall of the half-mad but very Christian and very clean Martina Dovino, in the small market at Escuenso, to collect his bunch of sorrel and his three leaves of sea holly. (We never knew how the priest managed to eat sea holly. The authorities had dispensed him from the daily three kilos of pineapples, on presentation of a medical certificate and a papal bull.)

He recrossed the bayou in the Tourniquet quarter, at the spot where, years before independence, the Fleming, Eyrickens, had tried to rape Estina Bronzario, and reached the foot of the cliff at Golzara. But, that morning, he didn't buy his usual stick of cassava from Nansa Mopata, another woman of God. The poor woman had to return home at the end of the morning with thirteen sticks, instead of the twelve she always came back with on Tuesdays. (She sold the priest one stick per day from Monday to Friday and two on Saturday; on Sunday, she gave any that were over to the choirboys after mass.)

'It's too bad! The world is changing so fast,' sighed Nansa Mopata, while the whole town asked itself what had happened to the priest to make him vary his usual itinerary.

'It's as if the sun had risen in the north and set in the south,' opined Lorsa Manuel Yeba.

'If they kill the priest, God'll destroy Nsanga-Norda by fire.'

'Don't be so silly, Estando Douma. God's like the sun. Whether you die, whether you cry, whether you're born, whether you scream out or hold your tongue, he always rises. His time isn't our time.'

In fact, no one in Valancia (or even in Nsanga-Norda, the bastion of the Mahometans) would have raised a hand against Fr Bona, the child of God, a man held in universal esteem and admiration. For all that malicious gossip had given him the unkind nickname of 'father of children of father unknown', and that Armano Yozua called him the 'white dragonfly', we all loved him, with a transparent love. We gave to him without stint. Years before, when the shameless daughter of Larmanso Kongo chose to fall in love with the priest and showed her infatuation by singing and dancing before him, we had to send the silly girl away to avoid a scandal. 'Go to Nsanga-Norda, the land of men whose flesh and blood are blind, the land of men who descend from the ape, not the dinosaur like us. There, you can love who you like without shame. Here, love is first and foremost a matter of honour.'

Before she left Valancia with her infatuation, she wrote the priest a letter which only the devil could have dictated to her. Fortunately, it fell into Fartamio Andra's hands.

My Love,
Who will ever know what the body is? My own, I feel, is

ready for all the follies in the world, is made only for excess. By God, alas! My simple body that only wanted to celebrate yours!

A body full of turbulence, with its domes, its spires, its cornices, its labyrinths, its machicolations, its minarets . . . And in order to dance with God, it takes by storm the soul's insipid sky in the instant of love that makes a mystery of the everyday body. In the face of love, God can only pardon us. Love of the flesh, you say? It is the flesh which, by saying 'I', transforms the universe into an endless song of triumph. I love you. There is hope in these simple words. It is the whispering of the universe. Hope borne like a fear. What love is not depravity? Christ's? Why did it kill him, then? Father! What body is not a mystery? I offer you mine in the same way Christ gave us his on the cross . . .

Accompanied by the judge and the mayor, Nertez Coma came to photograph the crime. Three photos altogether: the butcher's shop itself, the freezer, and the pieces of body. Trampled beneath the dead man's feet, we saw the priest's prayer book, spattered with blood and open at page 1,791.

The judge went round to see Estina Bronzario and asked her what she thought of the butcher's death.

'What do you expect me to think, Marcellio Douma? It's a death like any other death. Except that, according to the reckoning of the collar-bones, Elmano Zola should've died on a Saturday. He died on a Monday. He robbed his destiny of two days, which isn't at all bad.'

'Tell me, yes or no, was the crime committed by your women?'

'To say "yes" is a dreadful art, Marcellio Douma.'

The judge didn't know how to interpret this reply from Estina Bronzario. However, he held his chin in the hand that doesn't eat and spat not far from Estina Bronzario's feet.

'You can't spend your life saying "no", Estina Bronzario,' he said.

He turned on his heels and set off in the direction of the bayou, still worrying his chin. Estina Bronzario let him go. Armano Yozua called the midday prayer. We liked his deep bass voice. It reassured us that we were all still there, alive and real, waiting for the police to come. The mayor sent two telegrams a day to Nsanga-Norda.

Saudades: this was the last word spoken to us by Estina Benta on the day she went to meet her death. The clouds which, every morning, cleaned their teeth in the ocean, seemed to be repeating this word of sorrow. The cliff by Valtano, the lagoon, Jesus Island, Afonso, the tombs of the kings, the Island of Solitudes . . . all waited. We and they all knew that the police would come one day or one night. We would know who'd killed the butcher . . . And if not, someone would be found to answer for this crime. Lorsa Lopez would be put on trial for cutting up Estina Benta. We were in what Estina Bronzario and the women called 'the time of Estina Benta'.

The whites who were trying to explain the cliff's cry had established themselves on the Island of Solitudes. They were said to number eight hundred. Fartamio Andra do Nguélo Ndalo found this amusing.

'The time of the whites is over. Now it's the time of man. But how can one tell this to those white fools? They're almost as stupid as the people of Nsanga-Norda. Just think about it: like them, they descend from the ape. How stupid can you get? They've taken soil from the Island of Solitudes back to their own country to find out if the rock of the Quadrilla grows again like a tree every time it's cut.'

'They don't realise that a mystery is the best explanation in the world,' said Fartamio Andra, her younger sister.

'Let them look. They even want to know why the Mpoumbou rock north of Calcazora bleeds when it's wounded. The trouble is, the whites don't realise that they came into the world long after the world itself.'

'They think they're going to explain the cliff's cry with their Nsanga-Norda forks! How stupid!'

Armensah Fandra, the young epileptic widow who'd tried to warn Estina Benta the day her husband was to kill her, came to see Estina Bronzario to tell her that Elmano Zola, the butcher, or Salmano Ruenta might be about to be killed. She had returned from Valtano, where she'd gone after her first failure.

'Something must be done, Madame Bronzario. I'm sure they're going to be killed.'

Estina Bronzario didn't even bother to tell her that the butcher had

27

already been killed. She was to admit to us later that she thought the girl was just trying to draw attention to herself.

'Who didn't know that Elmano Zola had been killed? The world's full of people playing the innocent. I had to be careful, so there was nothing else I could do. In any case, between ourselves, who'd want to kill Salmano Ruenta, the town crier?'

'Don't say that, Estina Bronzario. In the face of destiny, all men are equal,' said Anna Maria.

Armensah Fandra went to ground after that. Fartamio Andra wanted to talk to her to find out whether or not the idiots in Nsanga-Norda were going to kill Estina Bronzario because of their obstinacy about keeping the capital in a place so rank only stupidity and hate could flourish there. Whether or not the police were going to come and take her alive. We looked for Armensah Fandra all over the Coast. We even sent emissaries to Valtano and Nsanga-Norda. No trace could be found of the widow, about whom in any case no one knew very much, except that she'd come from the Island of Solitudes a little before the time when we began to realise that Lorsa Lopez was going to kill Estina Benta. She was said to be the niece of Tipo-Tipe Mensah, the muezzin who'd preceded Armano Yozua at the Baltayonsa mosque, and whom we hadn't liked because of his sanctimonious voice. Mahometans, Christians, Martialists, whites, blacks, we were unanimous in deploring the lack of musicality of Tipo-Tipe's voice. We believed it could only call up the devil. 'It's a voice from the buttocks,' as Fartamio Andra do Nguélo Ndalo liked to say. Nature proved her right later: Tipo-Tipe was shaken by Nsanga-Norda fever and threw himself from the top of his muezzin's tower. 'Even God won't have pity on him,' Fartamio Andra had sighed when she heard the news of the accident that had befallen the most hated muezzin the Mahometans had ever sent us.

2

Sarngata Nola

On the evening of the sixteenth day following the burial of Estina
Benta's bones amid feasting, dancing and revelry, the air was rent with
a veritable tornado of bugles, cymbals and drums, mingled with the
coughing of saxophones and the braying of Nsanga-Norda bagpipes,
and interspersed with the ear-splitting din of explosions, gunfire, bangs
and rumbles, deafening janglings, and extraordinary elephant trumpeting noises. The sky over Nsanga-Norda was streaked with thousands
of artificial rainbows, flares and multicoloured phosphorescent lights,
and splattered with Nsanga-Norda fireworks that tore the leaden robe
of the heavens. Clouds of yellow, red and blue balloons rose into the
sky shaking their long tails of widow's feathers and innumerable tiny
tinkling bells. We were reminded of the time long ago when Estina
Bronzario's great-grandfather had also used balloons with tails to
release millions of gallons of artificial rain over the whole of the Coast
during the drought. The fiery purple throne that floated right across
the middle of the sky, drawn by seven giant balloons, made us think
of the Last Judgement. The throne glided slowly towards Valancia,
rolling on four Nsanga-Norda stars. We looked on the other side of it
for the seat of light of the Son of Man and the seven cherubim. We
looked for the throne of Abraham and the star of David as described
to us by Fr Bona. Then, because of the cliff's cry, we thought the Son
of Light would come out of the sea, between Baltayonsa and the Island
of Solitudes. We began to sing the *Magnificat*, our eyes turned towards
the sea. We looked towards Afonso, where according to legend the
seven hundred and twelve sages had leapt into the sea at the time of
the fifth contamination by the waters of the Island of Goya. We were
convinced that the babblings of Elmano Zola's younger epileptic virgin
daughter were about to be realised. This time, she'd said, the recapitalisation would take place in the sky. Then Estina Bronzario would be

29

murdered. It was she who'd predicted the murder of Estina Benta: 'On a Thursday, when you are about to celebrate the centenary.' And on the day of the murder, she'd gone to see Estina Benta to tell her: 'It's today.'

'The past and the future of mankind are in the sea,' said Fartamio Andra.

Martina Dovino, who lived on the buttresses of the cliff nearest the Nsanga-Norda road, spread the rumour that it was the police, coming to carry out their investigation.

'They're riding elephants and they're all dressed like princes of Egypt. Their clothes are shining like gleaming metal.'

'Ah! Very good!' said the mayor.

Estina Benta's bones were hastily dug up, scraped and washed, and placed in their former place, beside the axe used in the crime, the broken spade, the pick, the forks, the butcher's knives and the machetes. The pieces of sheet and the meat hooks were carefully replaced, as, too, was the piston gun which had been used to warn off anyone who might try to intervene on the day of the crime. Elmano Zola was put back in the freezer, exactly as the women (if it was they) had placed him. The message was reinserted between his teeth and the priest's prayer book was placed under his shoe-clad feet. Worried about his job and his chances of promotion, the mayor came and, with his own hands and the axe used in the murder, cut down the sign which, without the green light of the authorities, dedicated the square to the dead woman. With his own hands, he repainted the former name: 'Plazia de la Poudra', which dishonest hands had in the past always twisted and altered to 'Plazia de la Puta' ('Square of the Hooker'). The mayor changed the T into a D and managed, not without some clever acrobatics, to insert a half-starved R between an over-fed D and the A. But we could easily make out the two versions. It was obvious, though, that the mayor had acted without regard to the anger of the women (if it was they), who as a result bore him a grudge for forty-seven years, which was eventually to lead to his death in an explosion, the sound of which carried all the way to Nsanga-Norda.

Bugles and a great hullabaloo could be heard all over Valancia, setting the poultry cackling, terrifying the cattle in the fields, sending children scurrying and hordes of dogs running about barking non-stop, and turning heifers, kids, piglets and calves into a stampeding wall. We never understood why it was that in such circumstances even the animals avoided running in the direction of Nsanga-Norda.

The day following the cliff's cry, the sea had flung great quantities of lote and dead crabs on to the beaches and the animals had taken it into their heads – no one ever knew why – to run into the sea. (In the Tourniquet quarter everyone had thought this was the day when the sky and the sea would be joined together again, so they had all fled in the direction of Nsanga-Norda.) Many of the animals had drowned, while some had reached Devil's Island, north of Cartayonsa.

Behind the concessions, the song of the trumpeter birds quavered as they tried to contain their panic. Even those to which the shrewd thrower of binges, Lorsa Manuel Yeba, had taught the 'Marseillaise' now sang it so badly that, at any other time, the judge, who was fanatical about the 'Marseillaise', would have shot them on the spot. (The next day he saw the thrower of binges to tell him that his trumpeter birds were no longer any good at all.)

At nightfall, across the bayou streamed a long line of elephants from Nsanga-Norda, caparisoned in purple velvet, silk and silver, and surmounted with baldaquins. It was an incredible, mind-boggling extravaganza, followed by a human tide which made us think of the children of Jacob crossing the Red Sea.

'It's the recapitalisation,' sighed Fartamio Andra.

The elephants were ridden by men lavishly dressed in richly coloured garments, and they all had headdresses like the people of Karnak. The women were riding pure white ponies. The multitude applauded and laughed in their pleasure and simplicity. Diadems, necklaces, pectoral jewels, goblets and chinstraps shone as they were licked by the last rays of the sun. The brass band played the 'Valancienne', which stirred our perch-eaters' blood. (We'd never understood how the Nsanga-Nordans could bring themselves to eat meat; the people of the Coast had always eaten fish.)

'It's incredible! To think it's for this bunch of slobs, for these children of nothing, for these fools, these creeps, these loudmouths that we've worked like slaves!'

The mayor was disappointed. For, instead of the police, instead of the angels of the Last Judgement, we were witnessing the descent on our town of the ninety-three performers of the Sarngata Nola ballet troupe, which had been based at Valtano before the seventh decapitalisation but which, on the instructions of the authorities, had moved to Nsanga-Norda to entertain the capital and had become the authorities' own ballet troupe – fifty-nine women, twenty-seven dwarfs and seven pygmies from Oryongo.

The host of followers were for the most part fans of the troupe. They regarded making a commotion as their particular function and laughter was more dear to them than existence itself. Sarngata Nola had married all the women and had made the dwarfs sign a work contract with a clause requiring them to be castrated. The pygmies from Oryongo, as we all knew, weren't in a position to desire our women.

'The bastards have made me do all that work for nothing!' grumbled the mayor.

Sarngata Nola's women were beautiful beyond all imagining, and they danced the rumpus with consummate art. They were called the 'daughters of the devil' because of the salaciousness and earthiness of their boneless hips, which spat fire and made men sigh with desire. And since, at the time, Estina Bronzario's sexual curfew was in full swing, the dancers gave the men the opportunity to shoot their load in secret without any hassle.

Sarngata Nola, seated at ease in a purple and silver sedan chair, danced the rumpus with his head, smoked his *cachimbo* and ate *cancoillotte*. Full of smiles, he threw pieces of cheese to the kids for them to catch. They gobbled them down, only to spit them out again immediately. We were to discover that Sarngata Nola's *cancoillotte* contained very hot chilli and ninety-degree alcohol, because, he said, it was good for his ailing liver, paradoxical as that might seem.

Amid all this hullabaloo, and bitterly disappointed, we had to reinter Estina Benta's bones. The reinterment did not take place until the hour when Armano Yozua called the faithful to the sunset prayer. We helped Elmano Zola's widow put her dead husband back into the emergency freezer (the freezer in which he'd been placed at the time of the crime often broke down), fresh and still wearing the three pieces of his white ceremonial costume. This proved beyond all doubt that

Elmano Zola had been killed when he was about to set off for the town hall where, in his capacity as deputy burgomaster, along with the mayor and the judge, he had to attend the immortal ceremony of the raising of the colours. The judge had tried to persuade Nsanga-Norda to accept that he'd died in the performance of his duties, which would have allowed his widow to be paid the cheque for forty-seven francs awarded to the relatives of martyrs who'd died in the people's cause. Nothing doing: only the police could authorise the payment, after they'd completed their investigations.

'Let's hope they come before we all go mad,' said the widow.

'They'll come,' the mayor assured her.

'They'll come,' echoed the judge.

We all knew they'd come eventually, as they had when, some years before the second decapitalisation, the puppet, Ruenta Dalmeida, had killed the then mayor, Marsama Dibouka, and they'd taken sixteen months to arrive.

Sarngata Nola's troupe went to pay a courtesy visit to the butcher's shop. We all looked at Elmano Zola, smiling as if he'd only been killed the day before, and our ears heard what our minds refused to believe: 'They're going to kill Estina Bronzario, and then it'll all be over.' We regretted not having thought of putting Estina Benta in the freezer. Poor Elmano Zola! Frozen and covered in fresh blood, with the women's slogan gripped between his teeth by the ice, and still smiling his cattle-killer's smile. The three pieces of his body had, one could safely say, each died at its proper time and in its own way. If you moved the pieces of cow flesh, you could find the brass jar in which the butcher's intestines had been placed. His liver and his spleen were missing. We all knew that Estina Bronzario's women wouldn't have had the heart to kill Elmano Zola, nor the stomach to remove his intestines after sawing him in three.

Even during those days of the erotic sabbath, when delegations of women came and went, and came again, to tell Sarngata Nola that the time for women to be eaten by men was over, and that he no longer had the right to use his wives as sex objects or as instruments for sexual gratification, we all knew that, although their slogans were hard-hitting, the women themselves were soft-hearted. Proof of this was that they'd all wept in private for Elmano Zola and wore mourning for him. Even the artichoke-eaters of Nsanga-Norda, in an unwonted flash of insight, admitted that there was something fishy about the butcher's death. Some attributed his death to his stand in the affair regarding the transfer of the bones from the Harma Hozorinte cemetery to Nsanga-Norda.

'Greetings, Sarngata Nola! We've come to tell you that in Valancia the women are also men.'

'No, Fartamio Andra! My own wives won't be given the freedom to pass on lice. Please be clear about this, once and for all.'

Fartamio Andra shook her farthingale by way of a curse, and spat three times in the direction of Nsanga-Norda and four times in the direction of the sea, then marched off, followed by all the women who'd accompanied her.

We thought that, after such an insulting pronouncement, the dancer Sarngata Nola would find himself cut into more pieces than the butcher. So every day we asked the same ritual question, by way of good morning: had the actor Sarngata Nola survived the night, and had he got out of bed in one piece and on his two feet?

'He's a tough nut, is Sarngata Nola.'

'With Estina Bronzario to reckon with, no one can ever be tough enough. She's allowed him his night, now let's see how the day goes.'

'No, our friend Sarngata Nola is unkillable. They'll tell you so in Nsanga-Norda. They've tried.'

The multitudes that had followed Sarngata Nola in his flight from Nsanga-Norda had occupied land on the other side of the Tourniquet quarter and were building, at random, shelters which looked out to sea with an air of supplication that seemed to say: 'Not too much wind, please'. These shelters of mud and wood, with their roofs of all shapes and colours, were ill-suited to their function of keeping out the rain. As for us, we knew that the police would come and we continued to say so, in the hope that by dint of talking of the devil he'd eventually appear. The mayor sent telegram after telegram to the authorities.

'They'll come as surely as the Lord's day,' promised Fartamio Andra do Nguélo Ndalo.

They'd certainly come after the ridiculous affair of Manuel Koma's distillery, which had killed Carlanzo de la Cesa's fourteen brats.

They'd come after the mass suicide of the virgins of Yonda-Norte

convent engineered by the mad Artamio Sandra. 'We're killing ourselves so that the world will know that we exist,' they'd said. The
police had come from Nsanga-Norda on two further occasions,
although not even they knew why any more. As for their staying in
Valancia, that was now forever out of the question. Apart from the
fact that they often had nothing to do (in spite of Lorsa Lopez's crime
and the crime we attributed to the women, Valancia was a law-abiding
place), the police had it in for us and our town. The authorities had
never had time for us and our forefathers because of our obstinacy,
our constant rebellions, and our age-old belief in our local identity. As
far as they were concerned, we were children of shit who ate perch
while real men ate meat. They killed us, threw us into prison, gave our
flesh to the dogs, all to no avail. We were obstinate through and
through. The Portuguese, and later the French and the Spanish, had
tried to subdue this Coast of the devil. Sixteen times, the seven dozen
police sent to Valancia had disappeared in the same inexplicable
drowning accident between Afonso and the Island of Solitudes, while
they were fishing for conger eels. Independence changed nothing,
except that, instead of depriving us entirely of their services, whenever
their presence was required, the police came to us from Nsanga-Norda.
'In that way, they won't have time to go swimming in the lion's jaws.'

'They'll come and carry out their inquiries and depart the same day,'
the authorities informed us.

Alas, they had no control over the way things actually turned out. A
living example of the last defeat of the cops in Valancia was the mayor.
He'd been sent to inquire into the nasty affair of Elmunto Yema,
who'd been trafficking in industrial explosives manufactured from
sugar, nitrobenzene and nitroglycerine from Nsanga-Norda. During
the inquiry, the mayor took the opportunity to throw his khaki
boubou into the first available dustbin, for he'd fallen head over heels
in love with the young daughter of our brother, Almeyo Kansa. He
married her the same evening and, for better or for worse, chose to
remain in Valancia, and to hell with the police! The vicissitudes of the
attempts at policing our town had earned it the apt nickname of
Valancia-eater-of-cops.

Sarngata Nola was not intending to stay in our town longer than six
months. When Estina Bronzario told him about the murder of Estina

Benta and the whirlwind visit of the police, he held his chin, chewed an Nsanga-Norda pimento while his big eyes did a somersault inside their sockets, gnawed his moustache, and smiled.

'The police won't come, Estina Bronzario,' he said, his voice full of malice.

'They'll come,' said Estina Bronzario.

'You can cut off my left hand if they do.'

'I will cut it off, Sarngata Nola. But that's enough about the police. Let's talk about us women. You cart your wives around with you like provisions for the journey. You use them like kitchen utensils. We've never permitted anything so outrageous in Valancia. I give you seven days to free your wives. If you don't, you'll be sorry.'

'Do your worst, Estina Bronzario,' said Sarngata Nola.

Estina Bronzario shook her lace canions. Sarngata Nola gave a sinister laugh that made her jump. It sounded like the cliff's cry and was heard at the other end of Valancia. Some must have taken it for a trumpet call, for it brought crowds scurrying to the place where the crime had occurred. Here they waited, with their cloths over their shoulders and clutching their sandals in their hands. When Armano Yozua called the midday prayer, they left the scene of the crime disappointed and returned home in ragged groups.

'We'll go mad!'

'What was it?'

'Sarngata Nola's laugh, pure shit.'

After he'd laughed, Estina Bronzario gave Sarngata Nola some coffee. We thought she'd put poison in it. For two weeks, we waited to hear the news of the dancer's death. Mischief-makers tried to stir things up with their gossip.

'The women are letting Sarngata Nola off the hook because he has a tasty cock and a sharp tongue, even though he went further than the butcher, Elmano Zola, ever did.'

He trebled his dancers' salaries on condition they wore a splendid pink T-shirt bearing the disgraceful legend: 'I belong to S. N.'

When she saw these provocative words, Estina Bronzario ordered her women to intensify their sex strike and to rally more firmly behind her call for the liberation of Sarngata Nola's dancers.

'When they realise that it's our soul that brings them into the world, they'll force Sarngata Nola to free his wives,' said Fartamio Andra.

Estando Douma had grown rich and had left Valancia where, he said, money did not attract money. He'd gone to Nsanga-Norda, to live in the glare and shit of financial dealings. Since his screwing machines gave out after being used fifteen times, the men had reverted to living like spadefoot toads, given over to their shame because of the unavailability of women, who only rubbed their noses all the more in their misery.

The women sent a further ultimatum to the dancer Sarngata Nola, informing him that they'd be forced to act to protect their dignity as women. He only laughed his trumpet laugh once more, and set out immediately for Estina Bronzario's house. He avoided the bayou road, swam across the Rouvièra, not far from the seventh part of the bridge left behind after the decapitalisation, reached the railway line in the Tourniquet quarter, hitched up his trousers and his *gandoura* to avoid getting them wet in the dew, and took the bypass created by the women so they could avoid the place, upriver from the bayou, where the policemen had drowned. You might have taken him for some country bumpkin or a docker, not someone who'd become a local celebrity and, like Estina Bronzario, a great devourer of consciences.

He reached the house with his shoes heavy with mud and muck, and stinking of cow dung. Fartamio Andra invited him to sit down and offered him some tea, which he politely refused. She told him that Estina Bronzario was still asleep and suggested he have a drop of iron-water. But Sarngata Nola declined this offer, just as he'd refused the seat and the tea.

'Can't you wake Estina Bronzario up?'

'No,' said Fartamio Andra. 'The doctor has told her she must get sixteen hours' sleep a day.'

He stood waiting for three hours, his eyes red with impatience, anger and hate. His breathing became irregular. Fartamio Andra admitted to us later that she very nearly turned him out. 'He smelt like a corpse and his shoes were making the tiles dirty. He spat on the floor as if it were a heap of dung. I had to wake Estina Bronzario up.'

Estina Bronzario came out of her room wrapped in a sheet, which she held with her left hand to cover her nakedness. She was still only half awake.

'You've freed them?' she asked, in a sleepy voice.

'Stop being such a bloody fool, Estina Bronzario. My wives are free. Why don't you ask me about them before you piss in my face? I'm always ready to be frank about things even history's afraid to make up. You know Valtano. You know Nsanga-Norda. You know the Seven Solitudes in the rue de Nesa. I took them away from there, away from the disease, the hunger and the shame, because I can't bear the sight of women fucking for cash. I showed them how to make their cunts a cathedral, a holy of holies, the summit of heaven and earth. For the vagina, Estina Bronzario, isn't a Coca-Cola can or minced meat: it's the road all people must take to freedom, honour and dignity. The vagina, Estina Bronzario, isn't a come-rag. It isn't a fly whisk. It isn't moonshine. It's the will of God in flesh and water. That's what I've told my wives. They sold piss and pox, they were mere-sex, nothing-but-sex, I freed them from all the "that's what women are for" filth. I gave them a heart, a soul, a purpose. Thanks to me, they know now that the penis isn't an instrument of terror, a see-saw, or a juice-shooter, but our third eye. If you want them to be free to pass on lice and disease, you'll have to wait until I'm dead.'

He left as he'd come. The whole of Valancia soon learnt about the actor Sarngata Nola's latest insult, and trembled for his life. We knew that his crazy pride would soon make him one more reason for waiting for the police. We adored the actor, with the total, blind love of the crowd. It was partly because of the way he danced and his virtuosity on the bagpipes. When he was not dressed for battle, as he'd been on that day, he just wore his buskins and his purple velvet surcoat, which gave him the appearance of a Nubian colossus, for he was proud of his six foot nine inches. We loved his hoe-shaped chin, the fierce whiteness of his pearl-like teeth, his broad thoroughbred's chest, his hands made for gripping, wringing and breaking. His curly hair. Beneath his watercress moustache, his lips, the colour of new flesh, trembled with pure sensuality. Deep within his eyes, dug as if with a spade, gleamed a strange molten metal. The women called him Sarngata Nola the Amazing, because he danced the ninety-three rumpuses of the Coast with a faultless artistry. He was what our fathers had understood by the male: a man at the peak of fitness, voracious, inexhaustible, skilled in balancing dream and reality (hence a poet), skilled in trafficking his guts (hence a prophet, too).

When he arrived back home, Sarngata Nola drank three bottles of iron-water and went to sleep for the rest of the day.

Just as Sarngata Nola's ballet troupe had decided to remain in Valancia to await the arrival of the police, so Farmazi Benedict Bondo, who'd come to sell his iron-water, famed throughout the Coast, decided that he, too, would wait for the police.

'It's a strange business. I'll wait and see what happens.'

Elmanio Kanta, who'd come by sea, thought Estina Benta's murder a curious phenomenon and he, too, interrupted his circumnavigation of the globe by dug-out canoe to wait and see. Emilio Bayanda had been waiting for eight years. Caltazo Mundi had been waiting for sixteen years. The latest arrivals were Artamio Lacasa Loucy, Pedro Yota and the beautiful Afonsia Fonsio. Lacasa Loucy also arrived amid great pomp, with sixteen rumpus dancers and three griots, veritable walking encyclopaedias, who narrated the history of the kings of the Coast going back sixty-nine generations. They listed the twelve clans, the nine hundred and nine lines of descent, the three thousand one hundred and twelve families, without omitting a single genealogical detail. At the time of Estina Benta's murder, Valancia had had only three quarters left: Bayou, Tourniquet and Golzara. Now, with all the people who'd come to wait for the police, with those who were spreading the rumour that you no longer died there, and with all those who'd followed Sarngata Nola, the town had risen from the ruins of the decapitalisation. Whereas before we'd only had a hundred or so mulattos of Portuguese origin, now our blood became much more mixed, with Arabs, Indians, Chinese, blacks . . .

Beneath a sky as clear as desire, there hadn't been a drop of rain for nine years. But the invention of Estina Bronzario's grandfather continued to give us plenty of artificial water, except, alas, that it was too salty. An odd thing, though: apart from Calpazo Coba, the albino, no one died from sickness after the Thursday of the crime. People said it was the bones of Estina Benta protecting us. All of those who'd witnessed her death would also witness the arrival of the police.

The French who were looking for the atlantosaurus in the tidal reservoirs of Devil's Bay also came every other weekend to wait for the police. They said they thought the prehistoric creature they were hunting was the source of the trumpeting of the cliff that we'd heard on the eve of the crime.

One morning, the mayor rearranged Estina Benta Square for the eight hundred and twelfth time. We watched him put the bones back as before and, in their exact place, the instruments of the crime – the axe, the pick, the broken spade, the meat hooks and the machete. On the pick he hung the old elephant-leather jacket, eaten by time and tiny creatures (it had been a waste of time spraying everything with cresyl as a protection against the mice). Lorsa Manuel Yeba always came to help the mayor remember exactly where the deceased's bun was attached to the occipital bone, where to put the right hip bone, and to argue over the still disputed location of the left cuboid. That same day, the actor Sarngata Nola had found the two ophthalmic seeds down by the bayou and brought them back.

'What are you doing, Mayor?'

'I'm reconstituting the scene of the crime because we've just heard the sound of bugles coming from the direction of Nsanga-Norda.'

'I heard them, too,' said Sarngata Nola, lighting his pipe and puffing. 'But I don't think they're the bugles of the federal police.'

The mayor didn't reply. He continued to look for the xiphoid appendage and for the appendage of the left external malleolus, which he was, in fact, still holding in his hand.

'I have a moment,' said the actor. 'I can help you. Perhaps you'll reconstitute my crime after Bronzario kills me.'

'Do you really think Estina Bronzario could kill anyone?' said the mayor.

'They say she killed Elmano, the butcher.'

'The women have never killed anyone in this town,' sighed the mayor.

'But who killed Elmano Zola, Mayor?'

'Estina Bronzario is mad enough to use any rubbish that'll advance her revolution. You have to understand her: her demands need fuel.'

'What are her demands?' asked Sarngata Nola.

'Shit,' said the mayor.

'Can no one in this town give her what she wants?'

'The fact of the matter, Sarngata Nola, is that sex is like gold dust here at the moment, so everyone's ready to think her shit's inspired.'

The mayor laughed cheerfully. He continued his search for the place to attach the malleolus. Then the judge came running up to announce that the bugles they'd heard were those of the entertainer, Sarmanio Louti, who was accompanied by the Beauty of Beauties, Zarcanio Nala, and four rumba musicians. They were dressed in such absurd costumes that we were all too busy splitting our sides laughing at them to pay any attention to their hullabaloo without head or knocker (the word 'knocker' had replaced 'tail' in everyday speech after the former Madame Douma had decided, as a protest against her husband's screwing machine, to manufacture a knocker for use by women). 'Those fools from Nsanga-Norda can laugh,' said Fartamio Andra. 'Let them say what they like. They've been arse-lickers since the time of the Spanish. It must be hard to come into the world only to find you're an arse-licker!'

The group went to pay their respects to Estina Benta's bones and placed a bunch of Nsanga-Norda hortensias on the axe used in the crime. When everything was ready for the burial, the group performed their piece of pieces, a *Requiescat in pace* sung in the language of the pygmies. We began to like them. Sarngata Nola was so overcome with emotion that he embraced Sarmanio Louti, slapping him repeatedly on the shoulder, sniffing him, and licking his mouth as he might a lover's.

'Thank you, my brother, for singing with such soul, thank you for putting your finger on the profound beauty of things, thank you for bringing the world into the world and showing it its heart.'

Sarmanio Louti glowed like a laughing star. His eyes had taken on the colour of peace and the deep brightness of the world that can't be named. We were all drunk with this moment of puerile beatitude, with this moment of peace, the only one we were to experience in Valancia until the Resurrection. No one understood this pronouncement made, in English, by Sarmanio Louti: 'We have arrived. Sit down and do peace. There's no place sweet like no home.'

They performed their piece of pieces seven more times. We were quivering with a joy we'd never experienced before. The joy of peace. Peace of the body and peace of the heart. As if in a dream, we saw Sarngata Nola embrace Estina Bronzario and then, amid the

41

thunderous applause of the multitude, dance the rumpus of provisional reconciliation with her. The Plazia de la Poudra was given over to festivity and dance until nightfall, while the mayor watched over the objects of the crime with a religious devotion. 'As becomes his position,' people said. Lorsa Manuel Yeba danced the Nsanga-Norda rumpus with the Beauty of Beauties. He'd just promised to provide the whole town with all the drink it wanted for the celebration.

'It's wonderful to be a man,' said Sarmanio Louti.

This remark offended Estina Bronzario, but Sarmanio Louti explained what he meant and, while the whole town sang and danced, we learnt, to add to our joy, that Zarcanio Nala was not entirely from Nsanga-Norda, but had been born in Valancia – of father unknown, alas! – shortly before the crime. Her mother had died in Nsanga-Norda and had entrusted her sixteen-month-old daughter to Sarmanio Louti. From the old man's account, there seemed to be every chance that she was the missing Santia, the daughter of Larmanso Kongo, the beautiful stutterer who'd become besotted with the unfortunate Fr Bona and had been left with the vapid smile of a corpse following her disappointment. All her great beauty had been eroded, devoured and destroyed by her subversive love. Her body had dropped away, her cheeks had dried up. Her breasts, her hips, her belly – which we'd all seen the day she tore up the crinoline she'd worn as beauty queen, to put on a cloth soaked with Nsanga-Norda bird-lime and stained with the fat of the brown kite – had dried up and sunk to the bottom of her foolish passion, because she could only love what God had forbidden. Great floods only carry away stumps, says the proverb.

Fartamio Andra told the Beauty of Beauties the story of the passion of our sister Santia. She read her the letter left by her mother before she went into exile for love. The Beauty of Beauties was heartbroken, and cried all night and all the following day.

'You're a treacherous lot,' said Zarcanio Nala. 'The only reason for coming to this place is to find an excuse to kill!'

Her water-lily mouth suddenly tightened, her angel's eyes hardened, and the dream in her heart began to dance the rumpus of Nsanga-Norda. We couldn't understand why she announced that in future she would only answer to the name of Helen.

The day after the singers of the piece of pieces arrived in Valancia, a man, who was no more than an apology for a human being, came ashore from an Nsanga-Norda dug-out. He didn't lift his eyes for an instant from a big black book he was carrying. Its cover reminded us of the remains of the leather jacket left at the scene of the crime. Wherever he went, at whatever time of the day or night, his eyes were bent over his reading, except when he raised them from the book to fix them on the Beauty of Beauties, to whom he sang with his whole body and soul. The only other time the man raised his eyes from the black book was for the few seconds during which he breathed on to his glasses, the frames of which were made from salamander skin, and polished them with such agitation we just had to laugh. We nicknamed him Nogmédé, that is, the man-crab, because he walked like a Lebanese, but also because he said he could explain why millions of crabs had died after the bellowing of the cliff the day before the Thursday of the crime. The man must have been about forty, in spite of the large number of grey hairs in his thick mane.

He made the following rambling statement, which no one had the patience to listen to through to the end: 'It is written that a man will kill a woman, and that Valancia and Nsanga-Norda will disappear when the woman of bronze is killed. It will seem strange to you, but I found this book in the sea off Afa, not far from the Island of Goya. I was fishing for rainbow perch and sea-horses. I hadn't caught anything for three days. I was preparing to return. Ahead of me, I saw an enormous angler fish. It looked as if it was recently dead. You don't refuse the gifts of the sea. When I gutted the fish, I found a silver box in its stomach, and in the box, this book.'

'What a rigmarole,' said Fartamio Andra.

'I showed the box and the book to the crew of the *Calypso*. But they just called me a fool. At the time, they were raising the bronzes from the royal city at Yargo-Nonta. You won't believe me, but the characters in the book are made of magnetic photons, a technique unknown to us. It has taken me eighteen years to decipher them. The perch will all die, the humming-birds will all die, and so too will the crabs, before the murder of the woman of bronze. The cliff will bellow for the seventh time and the tree in the tidal reservoirs of Nsanga-Norda will sing its hymn in the Bamba language. Then the day will come when the earth and the sea will be joined together again. There will be sulphur and phosphorous storms, the gasses of Nsanga-Norda will reach such high temperatures they will liquefy carbon. There will be winds of fire.'

At the time, Estina Bronzario's sex strike was in full swing. The women had given their complete support to her call for the liberation of Sarngata Nola's concubines. 'A bloody mess which has lost us the opportunity to make children.' The men raged, whined and whinged without letting up, and went in serried ranks to Sunday mass to ask God, with candles in their hands, to have pity on them and to summon to his holy paradise the stinking mischief-maker, Estina Bronzario.

'She's stopping us from doing your will. She's stopping us from peopling the earth from the Gihon to the Pishon, from digging up cornalite stones as far as the land of Havilah. Make her die. She's stopping us from reconstituting the first flesh of man.'

They found new words for the Lord's Prayer, filling it with complaints, cowardice and platitudes. When Fr Bona heard of this, and when it had been explained to him why the women no longer attended mass, with the exception of Nansa Mopata and Martina Dovino, he kept the men for fifteen hours without a break beneath the arches of what had remained of the cathedral after the decapitalisation, and spoke to them as follows, in a veritable torrent of words:

'God isn't responsible for your silliness and he won't defend your cowardice. You were there when Lopez killed his wife, you allowed the butcher to be killed without even trying to raise the alarm. Gentlemen, I'm on Estina Bronzario's side, and so, too, is God. The vagina isn't an instrument for your pleasure or bagpipes for your spit. It isn't a depository for lice or a passage for squalid transactions. Try and understand what Bronzario means when she says the vagina's the Word of the Lord in flesh and water. You must realise that God doesn't help cowards. Cowardice is the very first invention of the devil. No, gentlemen, there's no salvation for fools. Salvation doesn't come cheap. True salvation is an act of heroism and faith. You must try and understand, gentlemen, that divine non-violence isn't inertia, it's an absolute violence directed against evil. The power of the light is a kick aimed at the forces of darkness.'

The men sent a delegation to negotiate with Sarngata Nola for the liberation of his concubines. During the three days and nights that the negotiations lasted, the actor kept telling them the same thing: 'What freedom do you want to give them? They sing and dance like your wives, they sleep and get up like your wives, they eat and drink what they like, and like the rest of us here they are waiting for the police. They won't have the opportunity to pass on lice, but they know what your wives don't know, and that is that freedom isn't just given to you, it has to be sought.'

My friendship with the Beauty of Beauties enabled me to get close to Nogmédé. He was in love with her and had for years been following her wherever she went to sing or to dance the Nsanga-Norda rumpus. He'd followed her to the seven towns of the Coast, from Valtano to Valancia.

'Love's a heartless and pitiless beast. Just blood and flesh that won't let you rest. Do you know, she throws my love back in my face, she pisses on my heart, but I love her all the same. Tell her this. You're a woman like her, perhaps she'll listen to you. I follow her with my heart which celebrates her body, which howls for it, which cries out for it, while she laughs in my face. Two years ago, at Nsanga-Norda, she was cooking, and my heart was singing as I watched her. But she saw me and flew into one of her rages and threw her cooking water into my face. Oh, God! When is love not loneliness? She has said unkind things to me, like: "Tell me, how'll you make me believe in your love? I know exactly what men are like. You just have to think of their water and you want to throw up. So stop pestering me." But she doesn't really know. You're a woman like her, Gracia. Tell her that love exists, that you can make something of it in spite of this infinitely monstrous existence of ours. Explain this to her, in a woman's words.'

A man's tears are stronger than all the wines in the world for a woman. His sobs are like cannon shots that tear our fragile being to shreds. I went back with him part of the way. We watched Sarngata Nola's troupe rehearsing, then we admired the agility of the engineers recently arrived from Nsanga-Norda, who were reconnecting the telephones that the decapitalisation had taken from us.

'I'm waiting for the police,' Varto Yansa said to me. 'They'll come, no doubt about it.'

The dying Zeluza Kosa, whose left side was crawling with Nsanga-

Norda worms, cried out in her delirium, and the whole town heard her: 'They'll come because this crime can't go unpunished.'

Even Fr Bona of the Sacristy, whose ageing voice was devoured by his chronic cough, always said at Sunday mass: 'Let us be patient, my friends. They will come.'

The aged Nansa Mopata, with her metallic voice exposed to the sun of her dying days, whose mouth could now only manage scallops, often said: 'I don't want to die until they come.'

The whole of Valancia waited, and trembled for Sarngata Nola's life. We asked ourselves all the time where, when and how he'd be killed.

Lorsa Lopez kept vigil over his crime. Apart from refusing to give his name to the square where the crime had occurred, the women didn't seem to bear him any animosity. It was rumoured that some of them even took him food, which he gave to his brother's, Lorsa Manuel Yeba's, pigs for, since leaving his pigsty, Lorsa Lopez no longer ate anything except Nsanga-Norda crickets, leeches, cockroaches, earthworms and slow-worms. We'd see him returning in his dug-out coffin from the Island of Solitudes, where he'd go to hunt for his food. He'd be reading a book which we decided must be the priest's prayer book.

Then Nogmédé told us that the things the murderer was making so much noise about were written in his book, too, in heraldic characters. The photons could be dispersed by blowing on them but, a few seconds later, the characters re-formed and resumed their original arrangement.

Day and night, Lorsa Lopez barked out the story of the Coast's end. A tiresome story, a madman's story, according to which the stones held mankind's memory and the whole of life's comedy. Thus, claimed Lorsa Lopez, you could read the long history of the Kattaratontes in the stones and the chalk of the Island of Solitudes. The Kattaratontes had lived on the Coast before the arrival of our ancestors. They were descended from the atlantosaurus. They were very tall people (up to ten feet). They were also called 'the human trees'. In their time, the week only had five days: two days for work, one for the market, one for a holiday, and one for prayer. They'd invented vessels made from magnetic light which took them to the moon and to the other side of a star which has since disappeared, called the padimontaurus moon.

'It's all a lot of drivel,' said Fartamio Andra.

One morning, the perch fishers returned with an incredible marvel. They called it the Motossé eel. When its metronome shaped head was landed at the tiny port of Vaho, the fishermen claimed (and they were right) that the bulk of the fish was still drifting on the other side of the Island of Solitudes. The whole day was spent dragging it to the shore. Lorsa Manuel Yeba brought his chain-saw to cut it up and the pieces were piled in three heaps. As there were still some pieces over, Anna Maria suggested they should be used to fill the depression caused by the cliff's cry to the north of the Tourniquet quarter. The suggestion was adopted. Lines of men (the women were forbidden to touch the eel in case they gave birth to monsters) carried dishes full of pieces and emptied them into the depression.

'That's done it this time!' We saw Lorsa Lopez hobbling towards the Plazia de la Poudra, where the mayor was hurriedly reassembling the scene of the crime. He ran on his one leg while the crowd gathered: women, children, men followed by their domestic animals, the old, the sick. You'd have thought the dead were about to leave their graves. The whole town was on the move. The mayor, unkindly nicknamed the gravedigger, was sweating under the mid-afternoon sun. He was hungry and still wearing his ceremonial dress – cross-belt, sash, decorations, silk gloves, satin gear and other attributes of his rank – as he was in the middle of marrying Fartamio Lanza to the delectable Emaniorita Canta (people were still getting married in spite of the sex strike) when he'd been told about the Motossé eel. Then, while the eel was being landed, he'd heard the seventy-nine bugles that Sarngata Nola's troupe were torturing to announce their bankruptcy, and had set off at a run towards the town square with his eternal spade. While digging the grave, he ruined his gold mayoral alb. The crowd, as usual, watched him as he worked. They knew he must be left to do the digging and restore order to the crime: the axe, the machete, the meat hooks, the fork, the pieces of sheet, the eternal left cuboid. He put everything in its place. The only lapse we'd noted during the last fourteen reconstitutions was that the mayor now added his own glasses to the tableau of the crime.

Salmano Ruenta removed the glasses to give them back to the mayor, while the judge, almost shouting because of the deafness that had overtaken him with his advancing years, said to him: 'It's not the police, Mayor. The sixteen cannon shots and the sirens are to announce a bankruptcy.'

'What bankruptcy?'

'The bankruptcy of Sarngata Nola's troupe.'

'Has Sarngata Nola been killed?'

His glasses slipped from his hand. His ears began to dance.

'No, Mayor,' said Salmano Ruenta, who tried in vain to stifle the laugh that always overcame him when he saw the mayor's ears dancing. 'Sarngata Nola's leaving.'

The mayor wiped his brow nervously and asked the crowd to do what they always did for the reinterment: cross their hands over their hearts, sing the *Requiescat in pace* in the version of the Beauty of Beauties' dancers, say the *Our Father* and the *Hail Mary*, shed tears, and observe a minute's silence, which was shattered on this occasion by all the banging and tooting of bugles, bagpipes, trumpets and fireworks. Estina Bronzario's women wept with great emotion, as if Lorsa Lopez was in the process of killing Estina Benta all over again beneath this immaculate sun.

Sarngata Nola arrived with his caparisoned elephants, his wives and his dwarfs. The minute of silence had to be re-started because he'd interrupted the original minute just as it began. But, during the second version of the minute of silence, the dancer pushed his way through the crowd, very quickly reaching the centre of the square, where he began to thunder: 'Stop being so bloody stupid with your bleeding hearts and your wooden words. Leave poor Estina Benta in peace. Stop using the dead to titillate your emotions.'

No one had the courage to call for a third version of the interrupted minute of silence. We were too upset by the spectacle of the baggage loaded on the elephants' backs and the wives' heads.

'We're leaving because people fornicate with destiny in this backwater.'

'Sarngata Nola, you can't do this to us!'

We begged them to stay, for the sake of our children, who could no longer do without their crazy goings-on, for our sake, too, for life would be dull without Sarngata Nola's utterances.

'Stay with us, please!'

We pointed to the army of children in tears tugging at the clothes of their favourite dancers. And to others who were breaking their toys in protest. 'Tell him to stay!' So the parents begged him to stay. We took him to see the corpses of two little girls who'd hanged themselves when they'd heard he was going, leaving these words written on the wall at the scene of their suicide: 'To the glory of the daughters of Sarngata Nola.'

The cortège of entreaties and supplications set off towards Westina, an unending flow of tearful faces, of broken hearts, of hands outstretched to heaven, of cries of consternation, of songs of commiseration, of eyes welling with tears. We reached the left bank at Golzara.

The crowds began to dance the rumpus of mourning. As the news of the departure travelled more quickly than the procession itself, the dance troupe found large crowds of people lining the route as they passed.

'Sarngata Nola, stay! We'll support you while you're without work. Stay! You've become the soul of our town.'

'You take me for a fool if you think I'm going to spend money I haven't earned by the sweat of my cock. Write and tell me when the police arrive. I've left my address on the walls of the Casa Vatio.'

The crowds came to the far end of Valancia, on the Nsanga-Norda road, and the first rocky buttresses of the cliff. Sarngata Nola was wearing his dancing costume embroidered with gold and encrusted with precious stones. He'd put on his enormous medallion and the broad sash of the National Order, his decoration as freeman of the city of Nsanga-Norda and his huge sombrero made from the feathers of the crowned crane. He sang the piece of pieces and lazily spurred on his elephant caparisoned in velvet and silver.

Then we saw Nertez Coma, the town photographer, hurry towards the mayor, beaming.

'Mr Mayor! Mr Mayor!'

Pushing people roughly aside, he waved a telegram for the mayor to see. When he found himself near enough to speak to him, the photographer whispered a few words in the mayor's almost deaf ear and handed him the telegram. The mayor read it, smiled happily and then handed the telegram to the judge. When the judge had read it, he passed the telegram to Sarngata Nola. The actor read it out in a very loud voice, laughed his trumpet laugh, then tore it up, declaring: 'The actor Sarngata Nola and his troupe weren't present when Lorsa Lopez killed his wife. So why should you expect them to wait for the police to arrive?'

'But it's an official telegram!' said the mayor.

'I wipe my arse with it,' said Sarngata Nola.

Then it was we first saw *him* approaching, as he emerged from the crowd astride his pitch-black Boulonnais horse. He was huge like a giraffe and wearing dark glasses and an olive-green leather suit. He had an incredibly bushy beard and excessively wide nostrils. His feet were firmly set in the stirrups and his jet-black boots made a clattering noise which set our teeth on edge. He dug his spurs into the horse's flanks and drew up alongside Sarngata Nola. Taking his left foot out of the stirrup, he laid it on Sarngata Nola's hands as he stroked his elephant, and pointed his hunting rifle at the dancer's throat.

'About turn, my friend.'

This was the first time we'd heard that voice in Valancia, the deep voice of Carlanzo Mana, issuing with some difficulty from a mouth buried in hair over six feet from the ground, from the centre of the face of a wild creature. It sounded like the voice of death. The hairs that devoured Carlanzo Mana's face were of abnormal size and length. His protruding forehead forced his dark glasses back into the enormous depression of his eyes. This man introduced himself to the crowd in these terms:

'Carlanzo Mana from the Ministry of the Interior. No one will leave this *v*ackwater until the police arrive.'

'Why don't they come?' ventured Salmano Ruenta.

The man gave him a look of withering contempt that turned up his lips and creased his forehead. As he'd tortured the word *backwater* in mispronouncing the *b*, we realised that he came from Nsanga-Norda, the home of those fools who'd never been able to pronounce the *b* and had settled for *v* instead. They were the sort of people for whom the issue of a free police pistol was preferable to study or farming. Nor was it surprising that Carlanzo Mana, from the Ministry of the Interior, resembled an oversized giraffe, or that he demonstrated to us, with so much talent, the abysmal mediocrity of the Nsanga-Nordans, who always treated everyone else like dirt.

Sarngata Nola's response was to aim a solid jet of saliva into his face and make it clear that he didn't intend to stay in Valancia now that he was bankrupt.

'That's for the ministry to decide, my friend,' said Carlanzo Mana, wiping the saliva from his face as if he were feeling a wound.

'They're a lot of asses in your ministry, if they take decisions without first checking,' said Sarngata Nola.

Carlanzo Giraffe, as the crowd were already calling him, took off his glasses. His eyes were strangely bloodshot. His mulatto's forehead took on the grey hue of a fresh corpse. The same colour spread to his neck, and a stream of blue snot began to run down from his left nostril. The man caught the snot with his tongue. This clumsy child's gesture made us all smile, but Salmano Ruenta exploded into a howl of manic laughter that made everyone freeze. We knew that he could never stop himself laughing out loud at something that made everyone else smile. A year or two before, during the minute's silence allocated to the bones of Estina Benta, he'd laughed fit to split his sides at the sight of the mayor's ears dancing with embarrassment (the thirty-nine police officers who'd appeared at the other end of Valancia had not, it turned out, come to carry out their investigation but to engage in manoeuvres out at sea).

'Even the Good Lord would've died laughing,' said Salmano Ruenta.

'What are you laughing at?' inquired Carlanzo Mana.

'Even the Good Lord would've died laughing,' repeated Salmano Ruenta, unable to stop himself laughing.

Tears were pouring down his face. His forehead was creased into two wide furrows. Carlanzo Mana leapt upon him and began to throttle the laughing man with his iron grip. We saw Salmano Ruenta struggling for air, just a little air for his lungs. But Carlanzo Mana squeezed ever tighter. The silent crowd began to cross themselves, then we heard a bone crack. The laughing man's tongue protruded further and further out of his mouth as he gasped for air. We heard another bone crack. Then a drop of fresh blood could be seen on his tongue, and the crowd crossed themselves with a sigh. 'Oh, God! How terrible! He's killed him.' The drop of blood fell on to the ground, at the mayor's feet. It was then that we noticed for the first time that the mayor was barefoot. He'd left his slippers among the paraphernalia of the crime.

'It's crazy,' said Artamio de la Casa.

'It's crazy,' echoed Lorsa Manuel Yeba.

Nansa Mopata said that Yogo Lobotolo Yambi's graffiti in what remained of Fr Bona's cathedral foretold the laughing man's murder, as well as those of Estina Bronzario and Fr Bona himself.

The crowd didn't dare leave the laughing man's corpse, which lay where it was, on the Nsanga-Norda road by the first rocky buttresses of the cliff. The corpse still held in its right hand the handkerchief with which Salmano Ruenta had intended to wipe his face when he'd finished laughing, the same handkerchief with which he'd wiped his face at the time of the Pope's visit to Valancia when, in the middle of the sermon, the mayor's ears had begun to dance because the Holy Pontiff had declared that God didn't hold it against Nsanga-Norda for being the bastion of the Mahometans. The corpse's right hand still held the bowler hat which the man had had to take off in order to laugh properly. The red ants were looking for scraps of food in the dead man's teeth, exploring his ears, his nose and his open eyes, which, we knew, were waiting for the police.

'Cover him with a sheet,' the mayor ordered, as the crowd began to disperse.

Sarngata Nola told his troupe to turn round. He tore the caparison from his elephant and, kneeling down beside the dead man, covered him with it. He placed his medallion and his sash of the National Order on Salmano Ruenta's body. He danced the rumpus of mourning for him and sang the piece of pieces. Nertez Coma photographed the corpse, then the crowd. When he tried to photograph Carlanzo Mana, the latter protested, showing his blue card. Then we saw Sarngata Nola burst into sobs like a child.

'I'm frightened of my ears,' the mayor said to the judge. 'When I look in the mirror and see them dancing, they make me want to laugh as well, like poor Salmano Ruenta.'

'What would the authorities do if we buried Salmano Ruenta?' the judge asked the mayor.

'Don't be silly, Marcellio Douma. You know perfectly well the authorities would be furious.'

52

'We could bury him at night, in secret, in a place only known to us.'

'The cliff would denounce you,' said Sarngata Nola, who'd been listening to their conversation.

Armano Yozua called the faithful to the dinner-time prayer. In the sky, the moon danced the silver rumpus it had always danced over the Island of Solitudes. The dogs barked at Death passing down the streets – at least, that was the intention attributed to them by the Nsanga-Nordans. We in Valancia had another explanation for why the dogs redoubled their barking when Armano Yozua called the faithful to the minor eight o'clock prayers: they were barking to commemorate the moment when Sacayo Samba had betrayed the Coast by eating the flesh of the salamander. Sacayo Samba had belonged to the Founders Line. His whole body had been covered from head to toe with scabies and he'd died a horrible death as the sores devoured all his skin and much of his flesh. We called his illness the Nsanga-Norda pox. Sixteen times, in his desire to kill himself, he'd thrown himself from the top of the cliff, at the same spot where Nertez Coma's daughters were to commit suicide; sixteen times the sea had denied him, refusing to kill him. He'd finally found salvation by throwing himself into the fiery mouth of Porta Indiano and, for years afterwards, people had thought they could hear his voice calling out: 'Will no one kill me? Death runs away from me.'

The next morning, crowds gathered in what remained of Fr Bona's cathedral, where, it was said, the Mahometan glyptographer, Baktiar Ben Sari, was going to decipher the message contained in the graffiti left by Yongo.

'No, sister,' said Fartamio Andra. 'I'm not going to listen to the pronouncements of an Nsanga-Nordan.'

But when Anna Maria told her what had happened, Fartamio Andra was forced to reflect on what Baktiar Ben Sari had to say. According to the Mahometan, Yogo Lobotolo Yambi had left his message for the whole of humanity, contained in seven Nsanga-Nordan words: *Lwenga, tiya sa tu-kwiza yizingi mutangala.* Which mean: 'When Estina Bronzario is killed, the fire will come.' Fartamio Andra explained that she'd already heard something like that. Her father had said the same thing with his last breath and, ever since then, Fartamio Andra, who was only twelve at the time, had remembered these words.

She'd known from her childhood that Estina Bronzario would be killed. It couldn't be otherwise. Estina Bronzario had to be murdered. We knew where and how. But no one knew by whom or when.

'She'll be killed by the Nsanga-Nordans.'

'Yes, sister, but the Nsanga-Nordans are as numerous as the grains of sand at Baltayonsa.'

We knew they would kill her. That they were going to feed her flesh to the flies. We knew with great precision that they were going to cut her into pieces like a sow. In fact, everything that the Mahometan, Baktiar Ben Sari, said about Yogo Lobotolo Yambi's graffiti concerning Estina Bronzario was known to us already, and he was merely repeating aloud what in our hearts we'd always thought. The glyptographer said, quite categorically, that there was probably also an allusion in the graffiti to Salmano Ruenta's murder, in line with Nansa Mopata's claim that 'the gods don't foretell the death of fools.'

'And where does Nsanga-Norda fit into all that?' Nansa Mopata inquired.

'The gods couldn't give a damn.'

'But, sister, you know very well that Nsanga-Norda will die.'

'It'll die, certainly. But there's one death for filth and another for the tough. And Nsanga-Norda can't boast of the death of a woman like Estina Bronzario. She'll die the well-done death of the flesh-eaters.'

On the morning of 4 July, the anniversary of Estina Benta's murder, Estina Bronzario slung her crinoline over her shoulder and, wearing only her petticoats and lace canions, took her slippers in her left hand and threw her brassière on to the visitor's bed by the entrance, behind the front door. She stamped the ground with her left foot, three times at the entrance to the house and three times again at the entrance to the concession. She spat a solid jet of saliva in the direction of Nsanga-Norda at the hour when Armano Yozua called the faithful to prayer, and set off.

'Where's she going?' asked Fartamio Andra.

'Who knows!'

'She's dressed for abusing someone. She's out for revenge,' said Anna Maria.

She crossed the bayou without lifting her petticoats or even her canions, which became sodden with water, got caught on the water lilies and trapped small fry in their folds. She walked quickly. When she reached the Tourniquet quarter, she raised her hand to her eyes to look at the desiccated cliff, whose scales and teeth were drying in the late morning sun. She wiped the sweat from her wet armpits with her madras. As the madras wasn't very effective, she used her fichu. At the town square, she glanced at Estina Benta's bones and crossed herself, without stopping. She had the sea behind her, the cliff to her left and, on her right, the lake. The enclosed valley of the Rouvièra Verda wound impudently between the first buttresses of the cliff. Estina Bronzario walked along the Rouvièra Verda as far as the former site of the Bridge of the Monoliths. She stopped for a moment to draw breath, turning round to gaze at the sea and at her daughter, Valancia: Jesus Island, the lagoon, the mission, the railway station, Baltayonsa, the Bayou quarter, the town centre, the Plazia de la Poudra, the Malsayo cliffs zigzagging into the sea and trailing small islands of all shapes in their wake, the lake with the shining silhouettes of its hippopotamuses, the old harbour with the carcasses of its wharfs, the menhirs and, beyond the menhirs, the burial islands, with the Island of the Angel showering its red water over a skewer of rocky loaves, all steeped in the millennial dream of a scrap of sky that seemed to dip its clouds into the water. Sea, sky and rock: they're the heart of us people of the Coast. Estina Bronzario felt a pang of anguish: one day she'd leave and join the rocks and the sea, and Valancia would remain Valancia, with its innumerable islands, its great-bellied rocks, its grandeur and its peace. She looked up at the sun, already so high and so brave in the sky, which had always dreamed the same dream as we did.

She spat at the thought of Carlanzo Mana. Blood rushed to her face as if she had a fever. But instead of scowling, she smiled. She stamped on the earth, which she'd sworn never to touch again. Carlanzo Mana had his tent at the entrance to the tunnel. The only land routes out of Valancia, the road and the railway line, plunged into the tunnel, then crossed the Devil's Gorge and its vertical heights by the Volmara viaduct (measuring two kilometres, the longest in the world). On the other side of the viaduct were the first dwellings of Nsanga-Norda. Carlanzo Mana gave his name to this part of our country because he'd maintained it by repainting the speed limit signs left by the soldiers who'd guarded the tunnel during the decapitalisation. A political agitator had written this insanity over the black lettering of Nsanga-Norda: 'Beware shambles ahead, maximum speed five illegitimacies per hour.' Carlanzo Mana hadn't thought it necessary to have the insanity erased, since his tent was on the left only for people returning from Nsanga-Norda, for whom the remark didn't seem to have been intended. When she reached the entrance to the tent, Estina Bronzario went to shake the bell that Carlanzo Mana had suspended there by way of a doorbell, but just as her hand touched the cord, a voice came from the tent: 'I was expecting you, Estina Vronzario.'

She entered. Carlanzo Mana pointed to a camp chair and invited her to sit down, offering her a piece of kola. Estina Bronzario took the kola, but instead of eating it she flung it in the direction of Nsanga-Norda. She searched among her canions and brought out her Commandery Medal and her Nsanga-Norda Star. She laid them out on her fichu, in front of the man. She took her Coast elder's cross from around her neck and began swinging it in her right hand. Carlanzo Mana showed her his teeth, reminiscent of a cutting machine, with a snigger that sounded like the whine of machinery. He made to touch the cross, but Estina Bronzario held it out of reach of his monster's fingers.

'You're an extraordinary woman, Estina Vronzario. What a pity you've passed the age for a man to get under your skirts.'

Estina Bronzario felt the blood pounding in her ears. She nearly sneezed, as she always did when she was angry. She coughed to get her voice back.

'Carlanzo Mana, you aren't a man, for the authorities have confiscated your balls. You aren't even a woman. You're a machine without a head or a knocker, a tool for digging up stupidity. You have neither pride nor honour. But that isn't my problem, since you can't teach animals what a man is. I've come to tell you that the next time you insult a woman in this town, we'll feed your flesh to Manuel Yeba's pigs, we'll throw your bones to the piranha fish, and your shitting authorities can come and do what they like about it. You insulted Fartamio Andra yesterday evening at the bayou. You struck her with that baboon's paw of yours – she couldn't hit you back, because she's only a weak woman and you'd have killed her like you killed Salmano

Ruenta. But I've come to return your blow in my own way. And here it is!'

She lifted her skirts and showed him her pussy, striking the ground three times with her left foot. Then she spat – twice in the direction of Nsanga-Norda and once in the man's face. Carlanzo Mana, who was drinking his *saccorrhiza*-root tea, filled a cup and held it out to Estina Bronzario. He broke a piece of bread and placed it on the cup, and over the lot he placed a piece of Nsanga-Norda meat.

Estina Bronzario ate the bread and drank the tea, but didn't eat the meat.

'You're an amazing woman,' said Carlanzo Mana. 'I must tell you, though, I'm not Elmano Zola. And even if I were, I wouldn't commit the *v*razen stupidity of getting myself killed *v*y a woman.'

Estina Bronzario asked for another cup of tea.

'How many sugars?' asked Carlanzo Mana.

'Seven,' said Estina Bronzario.

'A *v*lessed num*v*er,' said the man.

'A blessed number,' Estina Bronzario agreed.

She drank the tea, which struck her as being a little on the cold side. Then she gathered up her medals and her fichu, dusted her pussy, and left the tent. Carlanzo Mana escorted her to the sign on which was written the insanity. As he was about to grasp her hand to take his leave of her, he looked towards Afonso, lit his pipe and broke into a loud laugh, which Estina Bronzario was at a loss to interpret. Slipping his hand into Estina Bronzario's, Carlanzo Mana abruptly stopped his machine-tool laugh and muttered, almost pleading: 'The police will only come if you kill Sarngata Nola. Then perhaps we'll agree to let you have the capital back.'

'You have a good sense of humour, Carlanzo Giraffe,' said Estina Bronzario.

They walked a few yards further side by side. Estina Bronzario had her crinoline over her left shoulder. The man smoked his pipe. Their footsteps made a strange funereal sound. It was approaching midday.

'You can put your capital wherever you like. You can build it as big as you like. You can build it on a cliff or in the marshes of Balganza, for all we care. We're going to build the man who stands for absolute honour and dignity. We're the children of transcendence. We want to build the hope of dreaming another dream. Even if, as you said to Fartamio Andra last night, the vagina isn't a flag yet, we've decided to make it a holy place for the hearts of the future. Ruan Afonso's symphonies aren't sung to fools. I know that you don't understand these things. You're made to eat and shit. You're not interested in the heart of things. The only choice you know how to make is between eating and shitting. And sleeping. You think that's all there is to being a man.'

She shifted her crinoline on to her right shoulder and increased her pace. Carlanzo Mana tried to catch up with her but, finding that she was almost running, he gave up his attempt to follow her. The sun was approaching its zenith. Below, the arms of the sea were knitting the foam into a brown fabric around the tombs of the Kaonasian kings. The lake was rocking its brood of papyrus islands.

When she reached the bayou, Estina Bronzario decided to take a swim so as to consign to the Rouvièra Verda the animal smells that Carlanzo Mana's changes of mood had brought to the surface of her skin. She swam and dived and enjoyed the water, while on the bank her petticoats, her canions, her crinoline and her medals roasted in the midday sun. She laid her heart on the water's green limpidity, on its chalky smell and its salty taste, and revelled in the delicious contact with the sand and the coolness of its flesh, in the brown scurrying of the dace and, on the opposite bank, the dense flight of the jabirus. She enjoyed, too, the sensual lapping and gurgling of the water choked with peace, sighing, quivering and speaking with its liquid voice.

Estina Bronzario stepped out of the water and walked on the stones for the pure pleasure of walking. She chased the jabirus as she'd done when she was a child. (Woman of bronze, they said on the Coast. In those days, Nsanga-Norda and Valancia were one earth and one soul, a single sigh. It was not our duty then to hate Nsanga-Norda.) She felt her breasts: time had trampled them. The stones were warm. Crowds of insects had settled on them to sleep their reflective sleep. Estina Bronzario rolled on the sand, then on the stones, where years, many years, later she was to be cut down like a sow. She thought of Salmano Ruenta's body, waiting for the police on the Nsanga-Norda road.

Then Sarngata Nola appeared on the opposite bank, about to cross the bayou. She flung herself back into the water to hide her nakedness from him.

'Good day, Sarngata Nola.'

'Good day, Estina Bronzario.'

'I'm pleased you're staying. You have a grain of honour in your blood.'

Sarngata Nola passed so close to her that she found she couldn't cover more than a part of her nakedness, because of the limpidity of the water.

'You can swim with me, Sarngata Nola, before he kills you.'

'I prefer to watch you, Estina Bronzario.'

She stood up in the water and let him see her slender catfish's body. 'Here I am!' she said. Sarngata Nola thought how beautiful she was. He sat down on a large stone and watched her swimming until they heard Armano Yozua calling the faithful to the next-to-last prayer of the day.

'Did you know that Carlanzo Mana has come to kill you?'

Sarngata Nola didn't reply. He contented himself with taking Estina Bronzario's hand to read the fire in it. She let him hold her hand for a while, then withdrew it to put on her petticoats and her crinoline. He hummed an old Coast song.

> *If your body were*
> *not a mystery*
> *what would this world be . . .*

Fartamio Andra, who saw them return hand in hand, told us about a dream she'd had the night before. It threw us into a panic.

'They were just as I saw them in my dream when he killed her. Then the police will come and muddle everything up. Oh, the shame, my ancestors!'

'Don't be silly, Fartamio Andra,' said Anna Maria. 'Whatever else Sarngata Nola is, he's not a woman killer.'

'We said the same about Lorsa Lopez. We thought he wouldn't have the heart to kill her.'

Estina Bronzario had an extra place set for dinner. Fartamio Andra, who detested the dancer more than any of us, sat him facing Nsanga-Norda. Sarngata Nola drank a lot but ate scarcely anything. We thought he was sulking because of where he had been seated. We were to learn that, in fact, he couldn't have cared less.

'Of course, Nsanga-Norda is the land of fools, but why have it in for the land? What can the land do without men?'

'It makes men,' said Fartamio Andra.

'That's absurd!' Sarngata Nola replied.

'We've almost forgotten that we're waiting for the police,' said Lorsa Manuel Yeba, who, we knew, had spent the forty-two years of his existence in silent love for Estina Bronzario. But years ago, she'd said to him: 'Don't let's put the pepper of knickers and knockers on our friendship, Manuel Yeba. We'll love one another better without all that nonsense.' But he'd sworn on all the stones in the cliff and on all the water in the sea: 'Estina Bronzario, or nobody!' Fartamio Andra often teased him with these words: 'She smiled at you twice in a row, that's something. What more do you expect, a man with an Nsanga-Norda heart like yours?'

'When are we going to kill Sarngata Nola?' Fartamio Andra asked Estina Bronzario.

'When he chooses,' joked Estina Bronzario. 'We've never killed anyone without his permission.'

'I'll be killed after Estina Bronzario,' laughed Sarngata Nola.

Fartamio Andra got such a fright that she dropped the glass she was holding. Her red wine soiled the dancer's white surcoat. Sarngata Nola must have taken this accident as an insult, for he got up, excused himself, and left without shaking hands with anyone.

'I got such a fright,' said Fartamio Andra. 'It was exactly what he said in the dream I told you about this morning. The same tone of voice, the same note of pathos. I shouldn't have sat him where I did, for in my dream he had his back to Nsanga-Norda.'

'Stop imagining things, Fartamio Andra,' said Estina Bronzario. 'I know I'm going to be killed, but not by Sarngata Nola.'

'That's what we thought about poor Estina Benta. But let's talk about something else. After all, it's only other people who ever get killed.'

Manuel Yeba offered to sing us the legend of the sinking of the islands but, in spite of his talent and his goodwill, a gloom induced by the fear aroused by Fartamio Andra's dream had settled on us for the rest of the evening. We had good reason to be afraid. Fartamio Andra had dreamt about Estina Benta's death and had warned her to be careful. She'd been the only person to take Armensah Fandra's dire prophecy seriously.

'It's only a dream, Fartamio Andra,' Estina Benta laughed. 'I dreamt myself once that I'd turned into an Nsanga-Norda boa and swallowed Anna Maria. You mustn't make too much of dreams, Fartamio Andra.'

'Dreams are the seeds of reality,' Fartamio Andra said to her. 'I'm certain they're going to kill you.'

Another detail that made Fartamio Andra's babbling seem reasonable, and compelled us to think twice, was the fact that the old witch had predicted that the government notary who'd supervised the inventory at the time of the seventh decapitalisation would return to Valancia: 'I've resigned. They're a lot of fools in Nsanga-Norda. They graze on stupidity as sheep graze on grass.'

'Why don't you go to Valtano for a few months, and hide your life from them there?' advised Anna Maria.

'You're in the same world wherever you go,' replied Estina Bronzario. 'Murder accompanies you everywhere. They think they'll solve the problems of the Coast by killing me. They're mistaken. I'll be tougher dead than I am alive. They'll realise this very quickly. Alive, they can negotiate with me, but dead, I shall be God.'

3

Estina Bronzario

One morning, unprecedented crowds gathered in the Plazia de la Poudra, not to await the arrival of the police, nor to bury Estina Benta's bones, nor even to watch the departure of Sarngata Nola's troupe. The multitudes jostled for position to see the fish with the death's head that the fishermen, Fernando Lambert and Luizo Martinès Lopès, had just caught. It was a winged monster at least seventy feet long and weighing some three tons. On its hide, covered with scales, feathers and hair, gleamed the seven colours of the rainbow. From its eyes came a sonorous beam that reminded us of the fires of the great Nsanga-Norda cemetery. We couldn't make up our minds whether this really was a fish, or a snake. By eleven o'clock, people had come from Valtano and even Nsanga-Norda to look at the fish with the death's head. Fernando Lambert had baptised it thus because the creature's entire face was covered with kinds of black lenses and, on the top of its forehead, there were what looked like crossed tibias, which emitted a beautiful ray of light.

When Professor Mackall calculated its age by means of a process which completely escaped us, we were surprised to learn that the creature was three hundred and sixty million years old. Years later, scientists from the Queen City anthropology laboratory were to establish that the fish with the death's head was the indisputable ancestor of man. Crowds of researchers descended on Valancia – Americans, Russians and French for the most part. But no one could say for sure whether the creature was dead or alive. The scientists from Queen City thought it fed itself on protein which it manufactured itself from the light trapped by the kinds of dark lenses that covered its face and made it look like a Dogon death mask. We thought the event and the flow of strangers into our town would oblige the authorities to send the police, and that we would at last rid our collective conscience of its festering crimes. Some years after the creature's capture, the rumour went round that its flesh had the power to keep you eternally young if you ate it cooked in Nsanga-Norda oil. When the rumours persisted, the scientific authorities, in agreement with those of Nsanga-Norda, decided to build a fortress for the creature's safety in the former Olympic stadium in the Golzara quarter.

'In Nsanga-Norda,' the authorities had announced at first.

'Never!' Estina Bronzario had said, threatening to order the population to commit mass suicide in Golzara.

Then the scientists opted for Golzara for ecological reasons. The fortress was built very quickly. The authorities dispatched three battalions to ensure the safety of the fish with the death's head, as well as that of the scientists who were endeavouring to clarify the mystery surrounding the creature. Other theories were put forward, according to which the animal had lived during a period when we thought life on earth had been impossible.

There were three topics of discussion all over the Coast and even in Nsanga-Norda: Sarngata Nola, who was to be killed but no one knew when or by whom; the fish with the death's head, which was beginning to occupy an ever larger place in our lives because of the seventy-one thousand people who came to see it every day (this figure was doubled on Saturdays and Sundays); and Estina Bronzario, who was giving the Nsanga-Nordans, Carlanzo Mana and all our men a hard time and who'd come to symbolise the dignity and courage of the people of the Coast. All the towns of the Coast, and even Nsanga-Norda, had a Plazia do Bronzio.

'It's to try and make her unkillable,' Fartamio Andra maintained.

Nelanda, Marthalla and I were daughters of the same breast. Our mother died from thrombophlebitis only weeks after she'd given birth to us. Estina Bronzario suckled us and gave us honey water and one-day palm wine to drink. She'd shed few tears for her hussy of a daughter, who'd started going with men at the age of ten and whom she'd had to marry off in a hurry to safeguard the honour of Valancia's Founders Line. Armandio Bronzario's marriage was a disaster, and salvaged little of a situation that was in any case known to everyone.

When Estina Bronzario had noticed that her ten-year-old daughter's breasts were full of milk, that her cheeks were too round and that her eyes shone with a strange light, she'd summoned her to her room, undressed her, pinched her nipples, tasted the milk and shaken her head with incredulity.

'Who?' she asked her.

Armandio lowered her head and wept bitterly. Estina Bronzario set about hitting her until her hands hurt. She refused to give her anything to eat the whole day. But when evening came, she took pity on her and fed her as she'd done when she was two years old. She slept with her in her child's bed. For four nights, she watched over her. During the fifth night of her vigil, Armandio spoke Nertez Coma's name in her sleep. Estina Bronzario knocked on Nertez Coma's door at four o'clock in the morning. She waited until the door was opened and pushed Armandio into the house. 'Nertez Coma, I've brought you your whore.' Then she returned home. Two days later, a marriage was celebrated, first by Fr Bona of the Sacristy, and then by the mayor and the judge, Marcellio Douma. According to Fartamio Andra, Estina Bronzario attended neither of the marriage ceremonies nor the wedding banquet that followed, in spite of Anna Maria's efforts to persuade her to do so.

When our mother died, Estina Benta came to fetch the triplets at the request of her friend, Estina Bronzario, who refused to attend the dead woman's wake.

'Let Nertez Coma bury her where he likes. I'll ask him to give an account of himself when my sorrow has grown tired,' she said to Fartamio Andra.

'You can't do that to your dead child,' Fartamio Andra replied.

'The great of the Coast have always stood by their word, Fartamio Andra. I'm regarded as one of the great souls of the Coast, so I can't just be a woman. I've learnt to bang the table, and that's made me feel that I really am made in God's image.'

Since then, Estina Bronzario hadn't left us alone for a moment. We were, as she often said, three suns in the sky of her bruised heart. She was thirsty for peace 'with Nelanda, who resembles her for whom I shall always weep. I didn't even dare look at her corpse. Thus she'll always remain alive in my memory. Life is truer than death, O God of gods.'

'They're going to kill me,' Estina Bronzario said to Fartamio Andra, her ear-woman. 'Bury me without waiting for the police. Point my head (if they leave me my head) towards Afonso, and my feet towards Nsanga-Norda. At the bottom of the second suitcase made of Valtano wood, you'll find Sandoca oils and a dress made of *mandolivia* bark. Use these. Bury me in the cliff, under the fins of the fourteenth carp, between the fifth and sixth menhir, under the eleventh humpbacked whale. Cover me with six feet of earth and carve this on the stone: "She was ready to live".'

Fartamio Andra was very upset. Tears ran down her face, which was ageing at the gallop and taking on the appearance of a sea horse. Anna Maria chose this moment to announce something we hadn't so far been able to bring ourselves to tell her: 'Nertez Coma has given Nelanda's hand to Espansio Lola, the station-master's youngest son.'

'That Nertez Coma's a shit,' said Estina Bronzario, choking with rage. 'I'll deal with him before I die. I'll make a laughing stock of him. I'll brand his stupid blood with bronze.'

She planted Nsanga-Norda cress at the entrance to the concession and waited until it was nearly two feet high. Then, that very day, she sent out invitations to the mayor, his true-copy the judge, Carlanzo Mana, Sarngata Nola, Nertez Coma and five thousand others. We only understood much later why our grandmother was putting everything she had into an enterprise which was as surprising as it was crazy. Twenty-seven calves and sixty Nsanga-Norda sheep were slaughtered, hundreds of perch were fried, the throats of two hundred and ninety-one chickens were cut and, because of Elmano Zola's widow, who now ate no other meat except that of the guinea-pig, Fartamio Andra had been dispatched to Nsanga-Norda to fetch seventy-two guinea-pigs, which were strung on to ten skewers. As on the day of the abortive centenary, alongside the heaps of aromatic rice covered with multicoloured sauces, stood mountains of *foufou* and couscous. All Valancia was permeated with cooking smells, because in every house something was being prepared for Estina Bronzario's feast: yam stews, Nsanga-Norda banana-milk, *muambas*, skewers of fish, piles of crayfish, baskets of crabs, mountains of fried food, strings of sausages.

Lorsa Manuel Yeba, Manuel Yeba's son, who'd come, not from Nsanga-Norda, but from Yoltansa and was a true son of the Coast, not one of those bastards who have no notion of honour or dignity, struck his chest and announced: 'I'll provide the drink for your guests, Estina Bronzario. Do me the honour of not buying a single drop of iron-water. I'll get everybody drunk for you. They'll be crawling on the ground, and if anyone returns home other than on all fours at the end of the banquet, Estina Bronzario, you can cut off my right foot.'

'I'll cut it off if you lose your bet,' said Estina Bronzario.

And so we saw the old mission Chevrolet making its unsteady way towards the house, laden with case upon case of death-water, French wines, all kinds of alcohol and beer. More of the fields between the orchard and the concession than expected had to be cleared. All my grandmother's friends helped. 'Your celebration is our celebration, Estina Bronzario. Believe us!' For hours on end, Estina Bronzario received gifts and listened to and digested the women's eulogies, flattery and cajolery.

'Like you, Estina Bronzario, I've come into the world to love greatness. You know what it is to bear children, don't you? Inside, I'm a tigress, and they can like it or lump it!'

'I'm glad to hear you talk like that, Adimando Andra. They're going to kill me, and I know more or less when. But with my finger at least I'll have shown them the true heart of things, and something they can never kill by killing me: the stratagems and larger-than-life actions of a great soul of the Coast, because the fact is, Adimando Andra, that we don't come from nowhere. The earth gives birth to us. It leaves its mark on us. And because of this Coast, its stones, its cliff, its waters overflowing with magic and spirit, right up to my death I'll have been loyal as they'll never be in Nsanga-Norda, as loyal towards them as I've been to my woman's odours. And, after they've killed me, the three words that have guided my life, the three words that ought to be the motto of our wounded world – openness, solidarity, tolerance – will grow on my grave like couch grass.'

'Who says they're going to kill you, Estina Bronzario?'

'They're naïve. And the best friend of naïveté is stupidity.'

My grandmother increased the number of guests to nine thousand, among them Sarngata Nola's actors, the dancers of the Beauty of Beauties' troupe, the twelve Frenchmen who were seeking the origins of man in the island's chalk deposits, ten Portuguese, the forty

Americans who were hunting the atlantosaurus among the creeks and papyrus of Yolgora, as well as the Cubans who were guarding Fernando Lambert's monster. She asked her guests to wear the dress of the great of the Coast (purple velvet surcoat for the men, Valtano crinoline for the women). The members of her own family, descendants of the Founders Line, were told, however, to wear the white of Nsanga-Norda, but we didn't know why. At the time, the people of the Coast called Estina Bronzario 'the Lady of Bronze', or 'the Mucandi', that is, she who will be killed. We didn't know if they were going to kill her before or after Sarngata Nola, but no one in Valancia was in any doubt that Estina Bronzario would be killed. Perhaps one morning, under the loutish midday sun? Or one night? We had no idea. Lorsa Lopez had barked one evening that she would be killed down by the bayou.

Early in the morning, we saw the mayor arrive, accompanied by the judge. They thought Estina had revived her earlier nonsense regarding the centenary feast banned by the authorities.

'Don't worry, Mayor. They won't leave me the time for that. My grandmother, Sonia Bronzario, has visited me in a dream and told me that you'll soon be waiting for the police to come and investigate my murder.'

The guests arrived in happy groups, all smiles, clutching the thank-you packages they'd prepared for her. Some sang the piece of pieces, not for its meaning but because of its profound beauty and the peace that the song induced, because of the hope that it engendered, and because of the wonderful ecstasy and electrifying thrill it brought to the afflicted soul. Lorsa Manuel Yeba fired his arquebus as we did at Feasts of the Fish and at All Saints'. The shots drowned Armano Yozua's prayers. People arrived from all directions, a black crowd blowing horns, shouting, singing, cheering, converging on Estina Bronzario's house. Many hadn't been invited, but came just to shake her by the hand and put into her own hands the little something I-couldn't-not-give-you-on-this-occasion-the-last-perhaps.

'Stay with us,' said Estina Bronzario. 'I nearly forgot you.'

The number of guests soon exceeded ten thousand. The only guest who didn't bring a gift was Bobozo Inga, the sturgeon fisherman, who arrived at eleven o'clock in his work clothes, smelling of blood and roe. He went down on his knees, clapped his hands as a sign of deep respect for the Founders Line, then clapped them again as a sign of supplication (the Nsanga-Nordans don't know this sign and we'd always mocked them for this, but Bobozo Inga knew it for having lived so long in Valancia), and then whispered: 'I beg you, Estina Bronzario, call off the strike. I'm getting old. I must leave a child on this shitting earth, and if you don't call off your strike before they kill you . . .'

'The strike is over,' murmured Estina Bronzario, and the whole Coast burst into a great cry of euphoria that was heard in Nsanga-Norda. (We were, alas, to learn later the sad news that in Valtano and Yoltansa the people had misunderstood Estina Bronzario's intention and had celebrated the centenary by mistake, with the result that the authorities had set their pop-guns popping without waiting to find out the facts, leaving many dead and wounded.)

We saw men armed with bottles of iron-water arriving from all over, determined to celebrate the end of the strike by getting drunk. They threw their three-cornered hats into the air and tore up their stoles, scattering the pieces to the four winds. They danced, and drank from the same bottle. They set off fire-crackers. They flung themselves fully dressed into the Rouvièra Verda and wallowed in the sand and mud.

'Thank you, Estina Bronzario, you've given us back our hearts!'

Her neck securely sheathed in her ruff, arranging and rearranging her crinoline, Fartamio Andra, Estina Bronzario's ear-woman, felt all eyes boring into her. Then, under a hail of shouts and whistles, and with a hundred thousand heads nodding approval, she announced the start of the feast, after the traditional minute's silence for Estina Benta's bones, and the second minute's silence of hate and contempt for the 'pigs of Nsanga-Norda, who sold the land to the leopards as a slut sells her legs'. These two minutes out of the way, we moved on to the third, the minute of honour, which reminded our hearts, our souls and our blood of our fathers' promise: 'Men of the Coast will only love what is noble and great.' Then we moved on to the noshing, boozing and dancing competitions. Fartamio Andra read out the names of the entrants: Estango Leba, whose *curriculum vitae* stated that he'd eaten in Nsanga-Norda during the Independence celebrations; Omenanga Yonazi, who'd eaten in Yelum and Sordoma-Norda; Mallata Riza, as huge as two rhinoceroses, who'd come to Valancia to wait for the police two days after her niece's murder and who'd eaten in the north, Kezaria way; Bertani Zola, who ate to the sound of trumpets played by an orchestra of seven young women and who'd eaten hundreds of times at the Bolgerada fish fair.

While the noshers put on their singlets and warmed up in the ring decked with the colours of the Coast, Anna Maria read out the names of the entrants for the boozing competition. Three names altogether: Lansa Lossa Hamba, Culvato Cuenso, and Malconi Sènso, who, during a celebration on 11 July, had drunk sixteen bottles of *sowasilosuka*, four of *mataki-ntambi* and one of *koutou-mechang*. He'd died as a result and was only able to return to life nine days later after a rapid detoxification course administered by the doctors of the Cuento-Norta hospital who, at the time, could still attach the anus to the anus and the acromion to the shoulder. 'Not like your litmus paper doctors, who cut you up and then can't remember where the pieces go,' remarked Culvato Cuenso.

'You can't blame them,' said Fartamio Andra. 'The authorities sell diplomas instead of making people earn them.'

Before the actual start of the competitions, Estina Bronzario announced that there would be a minute's silence for Salmano Ruenta. 'After all, he, too, was killed by the stupidity and cruelty of Nsanga-Norda.'

'You're overdoing your silences, Estina Bronzario,' said Sarngata Nola. 'You really are overdoing them. Can't you give them all one between them?'

'If I'm still alive when you're killed,' replied Estina Bronzario, 'I'll give you one to share with that nonentity of nonentities, Carlanzo Mana, and then you can tell me whether the death of a man of straw has the same worth as the death of a man of bronze. Salmano Ruenta was killed because of his tic, Estina Benta because of her transcendence. Each of these deaths tramples on the other. Everyone in this village knows that.'

Estina Bronzario had never been able to call Valancia a town. For her, as for the majority of the women, in spite of its seven million insects, its coliseums, its bits of cathedral, its immense prison where

69

no one had been incarcerated since the seventh decapitalisation, its seven railway stations, its cinemas, its long-closed libraries, its capitols, its two tower stumps and its ten communes (Calbrozo, the Bayou, Sordoma-Norda, Cuento-Norta, the Race Course, Vaspora-Muenta, the Plazia de la Poudra, Jesus, El Nanza and Havilah), Valancia would remain a village until the end of time.

Fearing that the police might come while the town was caught up in Estina Bronzario's binge, the mayor, who was anxious about his renomination, had had the mourning flag lowered and the top cut off the sign that bore the dead woman's name. He'd left the spade and the pick where they were, in case he had to exhume the bones and reconstitute the crime in a hurry. We smiled, but without malice, because in addition to his own glasses the mayor had taken to including the judge's chaperon and stole with the objects belonging to the crime. He hung them with the left femur to the hook the assassin had fixed to the palaver tree, a thick, leafy sumac which had been planted, it was said, by the founders of Valancia. The tree must have been between seven and eight hundred years old. The authorities had tried many times to have it chopped down in order to end the belief that credited the tree with responsibility for the recapitalisations in favour of this accursed place, but Estina Bronzario had always waved in their faces the paper that made it the inalienable property of the members of the Founders Line. For this reason, we believed that one day we'd find her hanging from her tree, as Carlanzo Giraffe had promised: 'I'll hang you, Estina Bronzario, to save the Coast from bullshit.'

The rumour spread that the celebration had been organised to shame Nertez Coma and Carlanzo Mana. Nertez Coma, because he wanted to marry off Nelanda, and Carlanzo Mana, because he'd struck Fartamio Andra and told her that the vagina wasn't yet a flag. 'We'll make it a flag,' said Anna Maria.

We didn't even know what was meant by shaming someone.

Lansa Hamba and Malconi Sènso presented themselves at the finals table at the same time as Culvato was raced to the dispensary, to be revived and detoxified. Lansa Hamba emptied his seventeenth bottle. His opponent was one measure behind. The audience was jumping up and down with excitement: the Coast was ahead of Nsanga-Norda. People commented on the match, bet their wives or their fortunes, swore, surrendered their hands to be cut off. Sarngata Nola bet his savings.

The toothless Elma do Nonso, whose first three adult teeth (or 'surprise teeth', as we say on the Coast) had just appeared in his lower jaw, bet one of these teeth on the victory of Nsanga-Norda's son, Malconi Sènso, who was only a few mouthfuls behind in the sixteenth round.

'They're going to kill themselves,' said Lorsa Manuel Yeba, crossing himself.

'They'll stop in time,' was the mayor's opinion.

'What male can stop with all those women looking on?' said the judge. 'They're obstinate and will prefer to die.'

We heard that Culvato had vomited up his birth certificate and his heart at the very instant he was laid on the detoxification table. Estina Bronzario accorded him a minute's silence, but Malconi Sènso declared that he couldn't spare any time for the dead and took advantage of the minute's silence to increase his lead over his opponent. However, a little later, Lansa Hamba noisily swallowed his three equalising measures and the Coast exploded as one man in a deafening roar that was heard in Nsanga-Norda.

'He's a cock, so what do you expect!'

'Oh! They're both cocks.'

So the competition began all over again. We called out and shouted to urge on and excite the contestant wearing the colours of the Coast and his opponent, who was wearing the white of Nsanga-Norda – a white verging on a dismal grey – and looking our man, in his mottled purple, straight in the eye.

Eaters of meat against eaters of dace. Drinkers of creek-water against drinkers of iron-water. The north of the crowd sang, the centre hurled insults, the south was out of its depth. We gave vent to all the petty passions we usually took care to keep hidden.

'You eaters of termites, you bastards, you blockheads who steal the capital with the help of your pop-guns, go ahead, kill us, eat us, cut our guts open, but the Coast will always be the Coast.'

'To hell with all that rubbish about honour and dignity,' shouted the epileptic younger daughter of Elmano Zola, probably to take her mind off the pain revived by the anniversary of her father's death.

After their twentieth measure of iron-water, Malconi Sènso and Lansa Hamba both passed out. Their bottles stood there, like girls waiting for their lovers. We waited five minutes. The timekeeper counted to seven. A pity this number belongs to Nsanga-Norda.

'A draw,' declared the referee.

'I told you they were a couple of cocks,' said the exultant Nertez Coma.

Estina Bronzario handed the cups to the managers of the joint winners of the contest and asked Fartamio Andra to get the noshing competition under way. It was the turn of Lansa Hamba and Malconi Sènso to be carried to the dispensary, where they too died.

The noshing final was fought out between Estango Leba and Omenanga Yonazi, while Bertani Zola's lady musicians, disappointed by the defeat of their man, worried their instruments, producing from them a dreadful racket that expressed most effectively the unhappy emotions tormenting them. Most people were waiting for the insult-hurling ceremony and the binge that would follow. All throats were inflamed by the aromas coming from the iron juices, the sauces, the grilled and the golden barbecued meat.

The guests formed nine circles around the bronze dais upon which Estina Bronzario, Fartamio Andra, Anna Maria, the mayor, Sarngata Nola, the judge, Lorsa Manuel Yeba and many others sat in state. We waited. And those chickens that kept clucking! Because of the heat, some said. A bad omen, thought others. One of the chickens climbed on to the skewered guinea-pigs, jumped into the dishes of ground-nuts without eating a single one, and reached the heaps of yams that had been carefully cut up by the women with moon-shaped hands. The chicken clucked, and the bad omen theory won general acceptance. Sarngata Nola watched the hands of the women serving the *cagno*, lovely, delicate hands that knew how to knit the soul to the intoxication of the body, how to undo thunder, give birth to new worlds and invent intrigues – those agile fingers, those fingernails covered with nail varnish, that suppleness, that fire that knows how to give peace.

'What a beautiful poem are a woman's fingers!' sighed Sarngata Nola, while the multitude thought of the bad omen floating above its head.

Then Estina Bronzario made an extraordinary announcement, the meaning of which was known to her alone, and about which she'd said nothing beforehand even to Fartamio Andra, her ear-woman.

'Eat and drink to the shame of Nertez Coma.'

Everyone heard what she said, not least Nertez Coma himself. We knew that Nertez Coma had been married to Armandio Bronzario, who'd cuckolded him with the muezzin, Armano Yozua. But out of respect for the honour of the capital's ex-mayor, we'd pretended not to see. We also knew that Bronzario's daughter, married *manu militari* to Nertez Coma, had had a little boy who bore an outrageous resemblance to the muezzin but who, God does not sleep, died of pericarditis in his fourth year. Thereafter, Armano Yozua sang his calls to prayer with the voice of an ageing hired mourner from Nsanga-Norda. Then the triplets were born, who – it was said – looked more like judge Marcellio Douma than their legal father. At the time, Nertez Coma was a fisher of rainbow perch in the estuary, at Rio do Norte. We knew that the judge was the younger brother of Armano Yozua, the same mother, not the same father.

'What are you doing, Estina Bronzario?' asked Fr Bona, indignantly, kneeling before her. 'Estina Bronzario, you can't shame him!'

The priest made a rough sign of the cross over his ravaged old body, got up and left. All the guests crossed themselves. Instinctively, Sarngata Nola did so as well. Nogmédé came and knelt before Estina Bronzario, in exactly the same spot where Fr Bona had knelt, and begged her to leave poor Nertez Coma in peace; he'd been nibbled quite enough already by destiny.

'You can't do that to him, Estina Bronzario, for it's written in the Book of Truths as follows: "When the seventh decapitalisation has been accomplished, and the woman of bronze has spat upon the fisher of rainbows, the earth and the sea will be joined together."'

The mayor and the judge came in their turn to kneel before Estina Bronzario, begging and imploring her with one voice:

'You'll kill him, Estina Bronzario. Let the poor man keep his illusion.'

'Honour can't be negotiated,' said Estina Bronzario.

Nertez Coma was sweating like a pig. All eyes were turned on him, waiting for his reaction. We thought he'd leap on her, strangle her, and prevent her from dishonouring him.

'Father!' Nelanda called out.

Once more, there was complete silence. We looked first at Nertez Coma, then at Estina Bronzario.

'Why are you looking at me like a lot of fools?' shouted the man who'd become the target of shame.

The burning silence of our eyes drowned his voice. Estina Bronzario drank the contents of her glass, stood up, spat a jet of aspic saliva in front of her, in the direction of Nsanga-Norda, then sat down again. The crowd showed their disapproval of her gesture with a flurry of signs of the cross.

'Estina Bronzario, I hate you,' said Nertez Coma, in a voice dead with shame and anger.

'I don't hate you, Nertez Coma,' said Estina Bronzario. 'I'm branding you with the iron of my spittle to teach you to love that which is beautiful.'

She stood up, walked straight ahead of her, spat another insulting jet of saliva in the direction of Nsanga-Norda, and said to the multitude: 'Eat and drink to the shame of this man. I unmarry the daughter he's married to Espansio Lola, because that girl isn't his daughter. You don't beget children by trotting your index finger between a woman's legs.'

Nertez Coma stood up, smiled like a puppet, and left. We knew he was going to throw himself into the sea from the cliff. He walked as if in his sleep.

The formality of the unmarrying had been accomplished. That left the boozing, the revelling and the rumpuses. The rumbas, the boleros, the kamikazes, the *bamboulas*, the *pachangas*, the *yesas*, the *cannetons*, the *bongos*, the *yocayensas*, the *walas*. All the dances of the Coast, dances of the whites, dances of the Brazilian Indians, dances from all over. We could do any dance, we could.

'Estina Bronzario, I hate you,' shouted Nelanda.

She stood up, undid her heavy forest of hair, and set off in the same direction as Nertez Coma.

The crowd followed them with their eyes all the way to the bayou.

'Estina Bronzario, I hate you,' wept Marthalla. Then she, too, departed.

The revels lasted until dawn, in the absence of Fr Bona, Sarngata

Nola and Carlanzo Mana, who'd left. No one slept in their bed that night; everyone ate, drank and danced. The mayor and the judge drank and ate, but didn't dance.

'A great disaster is about to befall this town,' said the mayor.

'That's true,' the judge replied absent-mindedly, as if he was looking for a way round the mayor's prediction.

The days passed. Time seemed unchanging, slow, like a parenthesis opened up over the head of our town. And people gossiped. 'Nertez Coma didn't kill himself. Shame on him! What a disaster! How'll he go on living now? A life without head or knocker, mother!'

We all laughed at this man who, instead of killing himself, had simply handed in his resignation to the mayor (no more official photographer), to go and fish for rainbow perch in the estuary. No one greeted him any more, or ate anything he'd touched. His catch could only be bought by the people of Nsanga-Norda or Lorsa Lopez. No, we wouldn't eat the fish of a man covered in shame, nor drink the same water as he, nor wear the same coloured clothes as he, and if he walked down a particular street, no one could walk down it for months afterwards.

'Estina Bronzario, I hate you,' muttered the judge, who for the first time in years offered a comment that didn't echo the mayor.

It was Sunday. The people going to Fr Bona's mass talked about the man who'd been covered in shame and who – what a disaster, God of all the heavens! – continued to breathe the air of the people of the Coast. The altar boys had rung the bell twice. The faithful, candles alight and holding their palm fronds, waited for the priest. They waited until eleven o'clock, but still the doors of what remained of the cathedral didn't open. A group went to the mission to see if the priest was on his feet and to ask him why he hadn't sent Bertanio Moussa to open the doors of God's house. The group returned and told the assembled Christians that they hadn't found any trace of the Reverend Father Bona of the Sacristy. They'd opened the house and had gone to the man of God's bedroom. There they'd found his prayer book open at page seventy-three, candles lit before the bedside crucifix, a damp bath towel smelling of soap and scent on his bed, his toothbrush, shaving cream, lighted pipe, a cup with dregs of coffee without sugar and, in a saucepan on the cooker, a piece of calf's liver burnt to a cinder. In the wicker basket given him by our brother, Roana Loumoni, they'd found the seven heads of celery, the three tomatoes and the seven Nsanga-Norda pimentos the priest had bought on Saturday morning, at the time when Armano Yozua called the faithful to prayer. The sticks of cassava sold to him by Nansa Mopata, as well as the bunch of sorrel and the three leaves of sea-holly bought from Martina Dovino, lay laughing on the bench. But they didn't find the least trace of the priest himself, neither that Palm Sunday, when the faithful returned to the town in groups, nor during the three-month-long search for him that followed, organised by Anna Maria and Fartamio Andra.

The trouble was that no one in Valancia knew how or who to ask for a replacement for the priest, who'd arrived from Europe before the cliff's first cry and had come to love the Coast as we did; who'd seen four decapitalisations pass over him like water off a duck's back, but had never gone to Nsanga-Norda, the bastion of the Mahometans, a land branded a hundred times over by shame – after all, isn't shame a sin? At the vigil to wind up the search for the priest, for which Mahometans, Christians, occasional thinkers, Matsouanists, Kimban-guists, followers of the prophet Moze-Deba and a few not very important representatives of the Nsanga-Norda authorities had gath-ered at the mission, Nogmédé was in a state of great excitement.

'The Beauty of Beauties has shown me a kiss on her fingers. She had her back to Nsanga-Norda. Anyway! The priest's disappearance worries me because it is written in the book left behind by people endowed with seven senses that "after the disappearance of the man dressed in the violet of Nsanga-Norda, the earth will be swollen with *falmoufotans* (he didn't know what this word meant) and the woman of bronze will be killed." They're going to kill Estina Bronzario in a few days.'

And he read us a passage from his grimy book, which no one understood: 'At the hour for prayers, the disappearance of the man of God will take place, and when the muezzin has called the hour of solitude seventy-four times, the murderer will hurl him from the top of the tower from which he calls the people to prayer and take his place. When he has called Seven Solitudes, the woman of bronze will be killed. Then the murderer and his calling bird will be judged.'

'It's a lot of gibberish,' said Fartamio Andra.

We ourselves thought that the monster Yogo Lobotolo had carried off Fr Bona. This hypothesis fitted in with our belief that God created light, light invented time, time in its turn invented death, and death invented the solitudes: the solitude of Monday morning, and those of Tuesday afternoon, Wednesday evening, Thursday, Friday at the hour when Armano Yozua calls the fourth prayer, Saturday, and Sunday. This conception of things was bequeathed to us by the Portuguese and the Spanish, in return for the services we'd rendered their monarchs. For, in the days of our ancestors, the week only had five days: *Mpika*, *Bukonzo*, *Mutsila*, *Nkoyi*, *Bumungu*. *Mpika* was the day of rest, *Bukonzo* the day of the fish, *Mutsila* the day of the tubers, *Nkoyi* the day of the vegetables, and *Bumungu* the day of prayers. No one lived on their own. We were the Coast of the twelve clans: the people of Kwimba dia Mbakala, of Muvimba ya vimba ya mambu, of Kimgakia Kongo, of Mpanzu, of Mbembe, of Kingwala, of Bwende, of Sengele, of Kahunga, of Mpanga, of Fuma kia Mbongo, of Ngandu, of Nimbi, and of Makondo ma Fuka, the Founders clan. There was no shame then between the Coast and Nsanga-Norda, the shame brought by those who thought the capital had to be created by pop-guns. We ate aubergines, and the Nsanga-Nordans adored rainbow perch and chub. But then the Spanish came, and killed that time. We had to invent another time, outside pop-guns and muddle, and we got it into our heads that the sun could be made to get into bed at night with our petticoat bullshit.

On the eve of the ending of the period of mourning for Fr Bona, we heard that Lorsa Lopez had thrown the muezzin from the place from which he called the faithful to prayer, a sort of tower some two hundred and fifty feet high, built just opposite the old Baltayonsa mosque and which must have been standing for six years at the time. Armano Yozua didn't have many faithful to call to prayer, for he, his wife and his three or four female cousins were the only Mahometans living on the Coast. His calls to prayer were intended for his Nsanga-Norda cousins and Madame Elmano Zola, rather than for us.

'He bugged me with his noise,' Lorsa Lopez declared. 'Besides, his silence might now persuade the Nsanga-Nordan Mahometans to send the police.'

At the time, the murderer lived among the monstrous columns of the old prison, close to the cliff, which meant that morning and evening he had to pass through Baltayonsa. Perhaps he'd hoped to be able to forget his crime in that voluntary detention among the faceless concrete, the cold stones, the pensive bars, and the walls impeccably kitted out for punishment, with for sole companions the crows, the bats, the harriers with their thinker's heads, the barn owls, and the Nsanga-Norda jackals that came to lick his crime, giving him a vague illusion of punishment, and silencing with their barking that lugubrious voice that continued to batter his poor ears, making them reverberate day and night with the cry: 'Help me! He's killed me!' And the infernal parrot he'd tried to kill a hundred times, but which always managed to fly out of reach, screeching: 'Lice! She gave us lice!'

Early in the morning, Estina Bronzario learned that the two bodies had been found behind the cliff, near Jesus Island, at the very spot where, years before, Dominici Valansio had quitted this life in order to wipe away the shame which the Nsanga-Nordans had brought upon him when they dragged his wife away from him. She wept bitter tears and neither ate nor drank the whole day. She put on her mourning crinoline of Valtano muslin, painted her face with grey kaolin, and wet her feet with mimosa resin mixed with boa fat. She asked Fartamio Andra to pull out her teeth of honour, the middle incisor teeth of her upper jaw, which had been carved by our brother, Espancio Sosso.

She shaved her head, and the blacksmith, Fernando Manianga, branded her cheek with the star of Nsanga-Norda, above the mark of the great of the Coast.

'I'm not going to wait for your lousy police to come about them. Funeral tomorrow.'

Nelanda and Marthalla had thrown themselves into the sea to wash away the shame that Estina Bronzario had called down upon our father. With us, it must be said, conscience is a community matter; honour, too. The father's shame can kill the son, the uncle's shame can kill the nephew. In addition, as a result of Estina Bronzario's revelation (the revelation of something everyone knew already, but had kept to themselves), Marthalla, Nelanda and I were now just three bastards, daughters of father unknown, daughters of a slut, brought into the world on the back of sin and shame. Marked out by misfortune.

'Estina Bronzario has gone into mourning. Her sorrow is genuine,' said Lorsa Manuel Yeba. 'I'm also going into mourning.'

'They were so beautiful, gentle Jesus,' said Manuel Coma.

It was unanimously decided that the wake for the dead girls would be held in the Plazia de la Poudra. Throughout the night, Machedo Palma made mock of the authorities, so much so that people became scared. Elmoto Salvès tried to contradict him, but Machedo Palma never spoke in a vacuum: he produced figures, photocopies, addresses. He even went so far as to quote Da Colna, the Nsanga-Norda mayor's adviser on arcane sciences. He provided the menstruation dates of the mistresses of the Supreme Secateur, and the multitude howled with laughter.

After the funeral oration, which was read by Anna Maria, whose voice was so full of emotion she had to give it to Sarngata Nola to finish, we buried the girls in the customary way. Fartamio Andra spoke the ritual words and dropped the first handfuls of earth into the graves. Then came the farewell rumpus, songs, the firing of the arquebus, the piece of pieces, dancing and drinking – the best joy is that which is danced. We love our dead because we know where they are going. The joy you weep, express in movement, bellow, shout, celebrate with noise, that's the joy we've always kept for those who leave us.

The blessing was given by the Reverend Father Roguerio Duchemin, a big, handsome man, with an Nsanga-Norda beard, eyes full of malice and intelligence, a very large nose, red hair falling down over the nape of his neck like Valtano hemp, and the massive head of a man from the lower Dauphinois region of France. We were beginning to love him as we'd loved Fr Bona of the Sacristy, a man of feeling and humility who, like us, had never managed to love Nsanga-Norda, a land of bastards and centuries of treachery, the bastion of the Mahometans. Estina Bronzario had written the epitaph in her own fine hand and, reading it, the people tried to compare the handwriting with that in which the words given to the butcher to eat had been written: 'Women are also men'. They were the same words but it was not at all the same handwriting. Returning from the cemetery, the crowd stopped to look at the clouds of flies that were watching over the body of the man who used to call the faithful to prayer.

'You'd think they'd come now that a Mahometan has been killed, wouldn't you?' remarked Fartamio Andra do Nguélo Ndalo.

'Sarngata Nola and Estina Vronzario will have to be killed if you want the police to come,' replied Carlanzo Mana.

'What has Sarngata Nola done to you?' asked Anna Maria.

'Since his troupe of *v*uttock shakers has left Nsanga-Norda, nearly the whole population of the town has come here to witness your shambles.'

'The eye likes what is beautiful, and the heart likes what is heavy,' retorted Fartamio Andra.

That was when we began to think that Carlanzo Mana aka Giraffe had been sent to Valancia to kill Estina Bronzario and Sarngata Nola. Such was the monumental stupidity of the people of the creeks, who'd thrown their brains into their pop-guns and continued to confuse killing a man with killing an idea, in the same way that they confused the *b* and the *v*! So we got him to drink like a pig every evening, to try and extract his secret from him. We even invented a new expression to refer to someone who'd drunk too much: 'He's been on a binge of giraffes.' We all had a reason for hating Sarngata Nola: because of his origins (he was born of father unknown), his libertine tendencies (he ate the *umbra* and the mullet, our totemic fish), his first contacts with Estina Bronzario's women, and because he'd been at the root of the lengthy erotic strike. But we all loved him, with an identical love. It was the same love that bound us to the Coast, to its stones, to its brown sea and its mother-of-pearl sky, to its many shapes which always dreamt the same dream as us: the menhirs, the obelisks and temples, the field of recumbent statues. We loved its evening breezes, like the soft breath of a new-born child.

'It was through play that the dog ended by desiring its mother,' said Lorsa Manuel Yeba, teasing Manuelio Coma, the man we believed had originally passed the lice on to the dead woman. He was the son of another bed of the murderer's and, during the end-of-mourning rumpus, had danced with his maternal aunt, Yovoinsi Kebo, while Sarngata Nola was doing all he could to console Estina Bronzario. But the woman of bronze's sorrow was so heavy not even the recapitalisation of Valancia would have been enough to lift it.

'The body is made for enjoyment, the soul for reflection. The Nsanga-Nordans only have the body. As for the soul, they've never heard of it,' Fartamio Andra had said, the day we learned that Nertez Coma had failed to kill himself after his shaming.

The whole town pleaded with him to kill himself, because his shame could harm the Coast, especially now that the earth had resumed shouting its insanities at us. Every morning and every evening, a stream of people went to Nertez Coma to try and get him to kill himself, but he just laughed his laugh full of pain in their faces.

'Listen! The time when the sun fooled around has passed. Life's a challenge, and the most courageous thing is to live it to the bitter end.'

Estina Bronzario, who was more and more convinced she was going to be killed, wanted to bury all the dead, but Fartamio Andra persuaded her against it. That evening, Sarngata Nola went to see her and advised her to set up a local militia, because of what the Nsanga-Nordans were going to do.

'That's all they're waiting for, Sarngata Nola. They're just waiting for us to take matters into our own hands to come and put down an imaginary rebellion. Their trigger fingers are itching to do just that. I thought you knew, Sarngata Nola.'

'I wanted to see if you knew, Estina Bronzario,' said Sarngata Nola, draining the last drops of Nsanga-Norda tea from his cup.

Estina Bronzario chewed a pimento to retain her youth. She was right, it did, for we never knew how old she was, in spite of the many long years that had accumulated on her shoulders. Many thought she was thirty at a time when she was, in fact, fifty. One thing was true: we thought she'd live as long as her mother's grandmother – a hundred and seven years.

The Americans finally forgot the insults of our former President, to whom the guns of Nsanga-Norda accorded a moment of eternal glory every morning at the hoisting of the colours. They began to like our pineapples again, and to drink our tea. The Belgians resumed relations out of understanding, the Russians out of prudence, the English out of competence, the Germans out of modesty, and the South Africans by intuition. We began to plant again, not without trepidation, because those wrongly shaped heads of ours still harboured insults capable of putting people off our pineapples yet again. Estina Bronzario convinced us: 'Even if it's tourism and the sea that enable us to eat, we must put the money from the sea into the earth, because water passes but the earth remains. Don't do what those Nsanga-Norda fools do. They gather their fruit while it's still in flower: the best day is tomorrow. Don't do what those stupid Nsanga-Nordans do. They only plant pop-guns and think the pussy and the knocker are all you need to build the future.'

'The unseen world approaches at a gallop,' sighed Estina Bronzario, seeing Carlanzo Mana enter her concession on Good Friday.

We'd just heard the voice of the new muezzin, Sarnar Nesa Dalmeida Senga, sent by the Mahometans to replace Armano Yozua. It was a voice like a woman's, so he'd been nicknamed the man-woman from Nsanga-Norda by the Valancians. Carlanzo Mana stank of mescaline from a long way off. There was a gleam of despair and frustration in his eyes. Fartamio Andra motioned him to a seat. The man sat down and smoked his pipe so slowly it got on our nerves. Then he made this incredible pronouncement: 'Your Coast is just one great imvroglio. You're wasting your time trying to turn it into a no-go area.'

Estina Bronzario handed him a bowl of Nsanga-Norda tea. Carlanzo Mana took the bowl and placed it in front of him. He said his mouth and his stomach could no longer bear the smell of tea. Lorsa Manuel Yeba served him two fingers of mescaline in Valtano balsam resin. He added a few drops of Baltayonsa nepenthe juice.

'When are you going to kill me, Carlanzo Mana?' asked Estina Bronzario.

Bending double in his chair, the man stared at the ground. He began to strike the floor with his left index finger, in a pendulum movement. Then, in a voice heavy as bronze, and breathing each word with difficulty, he said: 'They can come and do this filthy murder themselves. I can't do it.'

He took an antique weapon of some kind from his knapsack – it was difficult to say whether it was a pistol or a primitive explosive device. From the same black knapsack (in the three years he had been in Valancia, no one had ever seen him without this knapsack, day or night), he took a bottle. The bottle bore a label with the inscription 'nitroglycerine'. He rolled the bottle towards Estina Bronzario's feet. Time passed, a frank silence that tightened the heart and set the blood on fire.

'They told me to reduce you to a powder,' said Carlanzo Mana. 'I killed Salmano Ruenta. His smell looks me in the eyes. His blood conspires with my blood. His flesh pours scorn on me, day and night. And they want me to do another murder. I'd rather let them kill me, Estina Bronzario, than soil my heart and hands in the people's flesh by killing your angry flesh. They'll kill me, I know.'

He got up and left, taking the road to Nsanga-Norda.

'The Coast is catching!' said Estina Bronzario. 'So, there you have it! Even the Nsanga-Nordans are beginning to understand greatness! I'll die with my pussy held high!'

We all went outside to watch Carlanzo Mana on his way to meet his certain death, for the stupidity of Nsanga-Norda doesn't forgive. His shadow made me think of Paolo Cerbante, my man.

I saw him again, arriving from Nsanga-Norda one November morning in the pouring rain, head bare, with a grim, unhappy look on his face. 'They sent me to kill Estina Bronzario, but thanks to their bullshit, I've met you, Gracia my grace! I love you like the world is tied to my navel. I won't commit their crime. I'd rather let them kill me.'

I, too, had begun to love him with the same strength of the navel tied to the world. With such strength! So strongly, it's impossible for me to put it into words. I had him in my belly instead of guts. The smell of love, the water and juice of dream, a small lake of peace the colour of the full moon – the great unending poem of the blood that celebrates in blood, the blood that strikes its fire against the wall of one's entire being, as the Beauty of Beauties, Zarcanio Nala, was to sing:

> My love
> You are the soiled dream
> That has never soiled me
> You are the infinite definition
> Of my finite being
> My little chest

Of dreams
My exhausted fervours
The other colour of my gesture
Thrown into the world by every world
The nameless pitching and tossing
Of that thought that loves us
That punishes us
That ends us
Your eyes open the door
To all my madness.

We watched Carlanzo Mana disappear, as he had come, astride his august beast. He looked back just before the bayou and raised his eating hand in farewell.

The great game of the soul caught in the blood's trap and suddenly beginning to sing each word, each gesture, to live every thing, and seeming to found a world inside every scrap of matter, under every arch of the spoken word. To show our contempt for the erotic strike, we went down the Rouvièra Verda as far as the Headland of the Russians and looked for a sandbank ready to welcome our souls and our madness, and there we celebrated the tumult of our bodies, the clamour of our senses on fire, the laughter of our taut-strung hearts, flung into all the fires of the world, scattered, liquefied, the one and only cause of the flight of the crabs. What love is not the denial of some sad reality? Under the scattered eyes of the stones, frantically we danced every bit of our male and female hearts until the evening, when our wild eyes began to fling stars into every corner of the sky. We were in the sand up to the sky, as Paolo Cerbante said. The streams that flowed down from the cliff all acknowledged us and gave us the greeting of fresh water. But as love is only fire, it's best to live it at water's level. My sun! My moon!

Seven days after the departure of the man from the ministry, Estina Bronzario received a message from the station-master. The note was written in Nsanga-Norda ink as the station-master hadn't forgiven her for what she'd done to his son: 'Madame Bronzario, there is a parcel for you from N.N.'

'I've no one in Nsanga-Norda,' Estina Bronzario objected. 'Unless they've sent me a bomb.'

That evening, we sat down to dinner at the usual time. We'd always enjoyed Fartamio Andra's cooking. She'd prepared Valtano-style fish eggs, cooked in *sofa* oil, with twists of chicken and meat in strips, pimento and vegetable stock.

Lorsa Manuel Yeba arrived and unloaded the parcel from his Méhari. He was feeling happy. Because the trunk was covered with the national flag, he thought the Nsanga-Nordans must have decided to acknowledge Estina Bronzario and were lifting the residence ban imposed on her at the time of the spitting incident. The vehicle was visibly straining under the weight of the trunk, which was heaped with flowers – lilacs, gladioli, Valtano gentians, anemones and carnations. We were puzzled by the death's-head moths we found in one of the bouquets.

'They want reconciliation,' sighed Fartamio Andra.

Lorsa Manuel Yeba's two salukis seemed to be lost in thought beside the splendid parcel. Lorsa Manuel Yeba asked Sarngata Nola and four of his pygmies to help him lift the trunk of beaten bronze from his vehicle.

'Who'd have thought it could be so heavy?' said Sarngata Nola in surprise, nearly falling under the parcel's weight.

'They want reconciliation,' Fartamio Andra repeated regally. 'At least I'll have lived to see that! I knew they'd come round to appreciating greatness in the end. They're returning the beard of the Christ of the Solitudes they took from us at the time of the first decapitalisation.'

Estina Bronzario sent for the mayor and the judge, who arrived at the gallop. They were afraid of the woman of bronze and thought they would come to grief because of all her nonsense about the authorities being after the hearts of the people.

Christ's beard was heavy.

'Let's eat first,' said Sarngata Nola. 'The trunk may be full of explosives. I can't get myself killed on an empty stomach.' Like everyone else, the mayor and his acolyte thought Fartamio Andra's cooking exquisite. Lorsa Manuel Yeba declared that such wonders could not be eaten without the accompaniment of a good French wine, and went back home to fetch some cases of *tuya* water and piss-a-lot, a few bottles of plonk, Bordeaux and straw wine, and a bottle of Nsanga-Norda wine. For the first time, we saw Sarngata Nola drink like a fish. He drank, sang, danced and ate Valtano cream cheese. Fartamio Andra sent for the Beauty of Beauties, who danced and sang the piece of pieces. After the weever eggs and the baobab sauce, we ate the birthday cake and sang Estina Bronzario the hymn to a long life. Encouraged by the alcohol, the mayor sang very loudly and off-key, in a voice which on any other occasion would have made us laugh. He was chosen to dance the birthday rumpus with Estina Bronzario, but declined. He was probably afraid that they'd be filmed dancing by a hidden camera. So the new muezzin danced in the mayor's place. We all had to acknowledge that he possessed the great delicacy of the people of the Coast: delicacy of heart, delicacy of body, delicacy of soul, wrapped together in a very fine intelligence. After the muezzin, the judge, then Sarngata Nola, danced with Estina Bronzario.

'Good!' said Estina Bronzario. 'Now I can forget my sorrows.'

She shone and sparkled in the light of the Nsanga-Norda lamps lit by Fartamio Andra. Fartamio Andra do Nguélo Ndalo declared that Estina Bronzario was as full of fire as she'd been when a quarter of a century old. Until the morning, no one gave any further thought to the parcel of reconciliation. The mayor and the judge slept top to bottom on the settee. The trumpets of the Last Judgement would probably not have woken them. The Reverend Father Roguerio Duchemin also slept, in an armchair because of his silly habit of wetting himself in his sleep when he'd been drinking. Nogmédé and the Beauty of Beauties slept on an Nsanga-Norda mat, forehead to forehead. Some of Sarngata Nola's dancers went on drinking, while they danced a languid rumpus and sang the 'honozorinate'. The Beauty of Beauties' actresses and the lady musicians of the eater, Bertani Zola, were dropping with fatigue, but didn't dare sleep. A few of the pygmies gave a concert of snores interspersed with the singing of the dancers, the judge's coughing and the tall tales of the oldest of the old, Fartamio Andra do Nguélo Ndalo. It was at ten o'clock the next morning that Fartamio Andra woke them for coffee and, chiefly, to look at the birthday present the Nsanga-Nordans had sent to the woman of bronze.

'Shit!' exclaimed Sarngata Nola, shutting the lid of the trunk.

'Shit!' echoed the mayor, who'd helped him to open the present, his eyes still heavy with sleep.

The Reverend Father Duchemin approached, and Sarngata Nola opened the trunk for him. The man of God crossed himself. We all crossed ourselves as we looked in turn inside the bronze trunk and saw Carlanzo Mana, covered in blood and wrapped in Nsanga-Norda muslin. His lips were parted in a big smile, a cow-wheat flower between his teeth, laughing his dead man's laugh. His hands were clutching a piece of pink cloth upon which were written in lipstick these words of horror and madness: 'Carlanzo Mana dies the death of Estina Bronzario.'

We were so angry we didn't know whether it was from shame or fear. We stayed for hours listening to the corpse of Carlanzo Mana taunting us and throwing clots of silence drenched in blood at us, as it lay there, cold, white and smelling sweetly beneath that disgusting smile of purple peonies and the unpleasant scent of Nsanga-Norda chrysanthemums.

'Who'll they kill after Carlanzo Mana?' sighed the mayor.

He sent for Nertez Coma, the fisher of rainbow perch, and asked him to photograph the body.

'Who'll they kill next?' muttered the mayor again.

'Estina Bronzario,' said the voice of Carlanzo Mana from the trunk.

We all heard it, but no one could believe their ears. We thought it wise not to make fools of ourselves by admitting to our neighbour that we'd heard the dead man's voice foretelling Estina Bronzario's death. Each of us thought our ears had imagined the voice, or that our unhinged minds had transmitted it to our unhinged ears. We were agreed about one thing at least – the dead man's lips hadn't moved. They continued to snigger with his last big smile, revealing his mother-of-pearl teeth the size of Nsanga-Norda maize, fresh teeth that breathed their whiteness from beyond the grave. Only they knew who'd killed Carlanzo Mana of the Ministry of the Interior. The corpse had been carefully shaved. Burial oils glistened on the skin of his forehead, which gleamed like the hair on his head. His eyes looked into the void. We wondered for what mysterious reason the man chose to smile his death.

'Leave the trunk where it is until the police arrive,' ordered the mayor, before withdrawing on his drunken, unsteady legs.

The Reverend Father Roguerio blessed the trunk. We noticed the same hesitation in his gesture that we'd seen when Fr Bona of the Sacristy had blessed the freezer in which the dead butcher, Elmano Zola, slept. We loved him a little more than Fr Bona, whom we tacitly blamed for having eaten the butcher's liver.

'The whites and their knowledge. Heck! They're sepoys, eaters of serpentine. They don't even know how to look at the sun any more. They live standing to attention. Roguerio's a man, as hard as we of the Coast are. But he still has his weaknesses.'

'All the same, Anna Maria, you can't call Roguerio a white. He has our great salamander heart. He eats and drinks like us. He pees on the street corner like us. He dances to his Good Lord just like the people of the Founders Line did. He doesn't try to hide his concubines from us.'

'Don't let's quarrel, Fartamio Andra. You always defend the priest. Let's think about Carlanzo Mana's corpse. It's starting to stink of decay.'

'The whites came a little late into the world,' said Lorsa Manuel Yeba. 'They danced to Bob's music, but didn't get much out of it. It's all Descartes' fault. He turned them into thinking machines. And now they can't be anything else. The poor buggers are made of concrete, stuck in an outlook that has neither head nor tail. God save us from the crude gimmickry of an existence based on mathematics, nitrogen and carbon! An existence dressed for going to town, ironed, folded in four, soaked with perfume. Streaked with weary hopefulness. Well may humanity thank them for services rendered, sister! – they've had prophets like Pizarro and Hitler! They've lost the sixth and seventh senses, and they refuse to come into the world!'

'We'll always spend our time coming into the world. No one will ever arrive completely,' said Estina Bronzario. 'I'd never have believed Carlanzo Mana would come to my place to wait for the police. Anoint him with Nsanga-Norda essence.'

'We've only got the theosophist, Larkansa Coma's, resin,' said Anna Maria.

Estina Bronzario disappeared into her room and re-emerged with a bottle of bronze juice mixed with Egyptian oils. Her face was full of sorrow.

'Carlanzo Mana, my grandfather said I was to be embalmed with this. I give it to you. If you've really died my death, I'll die yours when the time comes.'

Her voice shook with emotion. Fartamio Andra poured the oils over Carlanzo Mana's body. Then Estina Bronzario called for a minute's silence in honour of the dead man. Nine months after his death, Carlanzo Mana was still smiling the same mother-of-pearl smile inside his bronze trunk. His face had turned a metallic grey, his mouth was blue, and his eyelids as well. Under his chin, on the right-hand side, laughed the wound that had so carefully killed him. The muslin had taken on a powdery whiteness.

Then the corpse began to give out the fetid smell of an old wound again. Fartamio Andra doused it with resins and rare perfumes. Lorsa Manuel Yeba recommended the water and alcohols of Timbuktoo. There was only one other solution: block our noses with cotton wool soaked in Nsanga-Norda castor oil. Then Estina Bronzario ordered the trunk to be put in the garden, taking account of the direction of the wind. But the body attracted so many flies and insects that we had to improvise a burial without the knowledge of the mayor and the judge, who were terrified of losing their jobs, because Carlanzo Mana was from Nsanga-Norda.

Nogmédé came to the house to say that the death of the man from the Ministry of the Interior had to be interpreted as a clear sign of Estina Bronzario's own impending murder and of the advent of the day when the earth and the sea would be joined together again. He took the opportunity to announce his marriage to the Beauty of Beauties who, for the first time in the fifteen years he'd been courting her, had granted him a kiss, he said.

'Not on the mouth, alas! Only on the forehead.'

So, the Beauty of Beauties' marriage to Nogmédé was fixed for the first Saturday in May, the Month of the Fishermen. It was then March. Sarngata Nola agreed to be the witness at the marriage, and Estina Bronzario said she'd be the couple's ear-woman, if she was still alive.

'I must warn you that I can't close my eyes,' Estina Bronzario told Nogmédé.

89

'I'm not an apology for a man, Estina Bronzario,' he replied. 'I'm not a lie told to life.'

'Spare me your verbal virility,' said Estina Bronzario. 'Everywhere you go you sing that I'm to be killed. The whole Coast knows that. But you've turned it into a crusade. Who didn't already know that Salmano Ruenta and Elmano Zola were to be killed? Who doesn't know that they're going to kill Sarngata Nola? They have it in for us because of our special relationship with the truth. And because they're stupid, they think they won't have to account to the truth for our deaths. But truth will swallow them in one mouthful. They're people without souls, after all. What merit do they have apart from their imbecilic genius for fornication?'

'Dinner is served!' announced Fartamio Andra.

4

The Beauty of Beauties

'You were a fool if you thought I was going to marry a monstrosity like you, with your epilepsy and your stench of rotten fish, with your air of an unfrocked priest. You were crazy if you thought you could win me with word play as crappy as your hideous apology for a cock.'

She was shouting so loudly that the two choirboys put their hands over their ears.

The bridesmaids also put their hands over their ears. Unable to believe what he was hearing, the Reverend Father Roguerio waited for silence before repeating his question: 'Will you, Zarcanio Nala, take comrade Nogmédé do Sandoval to be your lawful wedded husband, for better or for worse?'

'No, Father, I won't!' shouted the Beauty of Beauties. 'The Beauty of Beauties doesn't marry an apology for a man who smells of Nsanga-Norda straw. I want God to hear me shout my "no" to him.'

There was a long silence and fire crossed as eyes looked into eyes, as faces sought out faces. The first words to be heard in what remained of the cathedral were those of our brother, Artamio de la Casa.

'It's madness!'

'It's madness,' sighed Sarngata Nola, taking off his witness's gloves, his plume of honour and his Nsanga-Norda cardigan made from condor feathers.

Lorsa Manuel Yeba declared that he was offering a binge to all those who wanted to forget this madness.

The Reverend Father Roguerio's nose and cheeks were bright red. He didn't know how to handle Zarcanio Nala's scandalous behaviour. Was she made in the image of man or of God? The priest crossed himself and, closing the prayer book, took off his biretta and his cassock, and washed his hands, drying them on the end of his surplice. Then he asked the faithful to leave, without giving them the customary blessing. Everyone trooped off to Lorsa Manuel Yeba's house for the promised binge.

Only Nogmédé remained kneeling in the cathedral, his hands covering his disgraced member. He was celebrating his marriage to shame and humiliation. He remained in that position for months, until one day Fartamio Andra came and anointed him with the oils of the theosophist, Larkansa Coma, because he was beginning to stink and maggots were coming out of his mouth, his ears and his nostrils. We watched these eaters of the dead while the Reverend Father Roguerio celebrated the Christmas mass. We wondered what the police would find left of the kneeling body spreading maggots throughout what remained of the cathedral. The clothes, which had become too big, hung about the body in dry, stiff shapes. The skin had shrunk over the skull. The bones of the arms gave the whole a sad appearance of caricature, while the teeth laughed a big laugh of dead stone. The hands still held the big floppy beret of printed organdie. There are so many things that words cannot say, alas! We saw them.

Estina Bronzario had sent us, Fartamio Andra and me, to lay flowers on the graves of Nelanda and Marthalla. She'd never been able to bring herself to look at the mounds of earth which now replaced the joy of living that had once inhabited the two sisters. Sarngata Nola went with us, but he refused to go as far as the graves. He, too, hated the sight of the stone-covered mounds lying proudly silent under the tree of the Founders Line.

When we returned that evening, at the time when Nogmédé used to come and tell us that the Beauty of Beauties had given him a kiss or a smile, we found Estina Bronzario in tears. Sarngata Nola tried to console her. She didn't stop crying. We thought at first it was remorse for the loss of Nelanda and Marthalla. Then she explained that when she'd fallen asleep for a few minutes during the afternoon, she'd seen her corpse in a dream.

'What wickedness, my ancestors! They'd cut me up like mutton.' (Her voice made a boring sound, as if she were whistling.) 'That corpse! What a horror of nature! A night and a challenge. Do you realise, Fartamio Andra, they're going to cut me up and I won't even have the means to thank them! Nor even to hurl my contempt at them!'

She began to pray aloud, as if we'd ceased to exist for her.

'God, how difficult it is to leave this flesh with which we've had so many dreams! The honour of knowing that in the end one is no more than a saltless corpse. God! What ugliness is man!'

We hadn't forgotten the scandal of the Beauty of Beauties' rejection of Nogmédé. The whole town was still talking about it, commenting, judging, analysing, always arriving at the same conclusion that had been reached by our brother, Artamio de la Casa: it was madness! We couldn't understand why Zarcanio Nala had torn up her wedding crinoline and was now wearing Nsanga-Norda white, and had chosen the name of Helen for her period of mourning.

'When they kill me, bury me on the Nsanga-Norda road, between the tunnel exit and the viaduct. If you can.'

'You are ageing aloud, Estina Bronzario,' said Sarngata Nola.

'The only way to avoid utterly shaming your corpse is to settle your account with life with complete honesty. You can't tell truth what shape to give your nose, Sarngata Nola. When vanity has passed, man is all that is left. Absolute nothingness, standing before God. The nothingness that pisses in the streets.'

She smiled. A smile full of indulgence. Sarngata Nola kissed her on the forehead, took her left hand, and looked at her in the same way one reads a book.

'Man only has words to say what even words can't say,' said Estina Bronzario. 'He only has words to help him to live.'

Her voice danced the rumpus of Nsanga-Norda. Only her heart knew. Even Sarngata Nola's voice, which had always laughed and danced, began to falter. Fartamio Andra brought us pieces of kola, and a pimento for Estina Bronzario. The sound of crunching was so ugly! No one went to sleep before Estina Bronzario that night. At around three o'clock in the morning, my man got up, irritated, he said, 'by your stupidity in staying here like ant-hills, doing nothing, saying nothing, as if you're waiting for someone to come.'

At the time, a piece of news was doing the rounds of Valancia's ears: the Beauty of Beauties, it was said, knew who'd given the lice to Estina Benta, who'd told Lorsa Lopez, and when Lorsa Lopez had finally decided to commit his crime.

'She didn't tell anyone, just to get her own back.'

'Isn't that so, sister?'

'She won't say anything until after Estina Bronzario has been murdered.'

Everyone tried to get close to her, inviting her to dinner or for a drink, to try and get her secret out of her. Fartamio Andra invited her for a meal on Shrove Tuesday and plucked up courage to ask her if what people were saying was true.

'It's all rubbish, my sister. I only know one thing: they're going to kill Estina Bronzario. I even wonder if they've not already killed her.'

When Fartamio Andra told her that the Beauty of Beauties thought they'd already killed her, Estina Bronzario smiled, the same smile she'd smiled years before, that evening when Sarngata Nola had sworn that the police wouldn't come and had offered to let her cut off his hand.

'Give me your hand, Sarngata Nola, so that I can cut it off before they kill me.'

Laughing, Sarngata Nola gave her his hand. She kissed it. They sang as they danced the rumpus, while Manuel Yeba beat the edge of the table like a drum and Fartamio Andra played the flute with the stem of her enormous pipe. Then, as usual, Manuel Yeba rushed home and came back with a heavy case of iron-juice, inviting the neighbours to join in the binge. The next morning, at the hour when the man-woman called the faithful to prayer, Aunt Mangala, who lived in the Tourni-quet quarter, turned up at the house in tears.

'I've come because they're saying the Nsanga-Nordans are going to kill Estina Bronzario.'

Then Sarngata Nola got up and blew his horn to call his dancers and pygmies together. Mounting his Boulonnais horse, he spoke as follows: 'We live in a land of stone so, to prevent them from killing Estina Bronzario, I call on you to build a stone monster – a citadel. There, we'll hide Estina Bronzario, two hundred cubits up, to keep her safe from the death they've destined her for. Come, friends, ours are not the boxed hearts of the Nsanga-Nordans.'

He and Lorsa Manuel Yeba traced the outline of the citadel on the seventh buttress of the cliff. The multitude set about bringing stones. Soon, the place was turned into an immense building site, sending up clouds of variegated dust, day and night, amidst an incredible din and the singing of songs from all over the Coast.

'What are you doing, Sarngata Nola?' the mayor and the judge demanded to know.

'Building a citadel,' said Sarngata Nola.

The mayor and his acolyte took this reply as a joke, in spite of the evidence of the multitudes carrying, breaking and polishing stones. The trenches dug by Sarngata Nola's men had to be forty feet wide and sixteen feet deep. Lines of people carried the earth away in the opposite direction to those who were bringing the stones, rolling them, pushing them, and pulling them on logs. Others went and threw the clay into the sea, on the side by the blue cliff, at the place from where, according to tradition, Nertez Coma should have thrown himself after the ceremony of unmarrying. All of Sarngata Nola's actors dug along with him, singing the piece of pieces.

'What's all this hullabaloo?'

'Sarngata Nola is building a citadel to prevent them from killing the woman of bronze.'

'And how are the authorities going to take it?'

'Well, sister, the authorities have never denied Sarngata Nola anything. They'll leave him alone.'

'What a silly idea, a citadel.'

But the stone monster grew. It could already be seen from Nsanga-Norda. For sixteen years, day and night, the black crowds rolled the huge boulders, singing and dancing the rumpus of hope. Month after month, year after year, the edifice rose into the blue sky, to which the stones showed their fierce shapes and the inexhaustible dream of men. At the end of the sixteenth year, the stone monster had attained the unimaginable height of one thousand four hundred feet. While Estina Bronzario smiled her wise old woman's smile, the Coast brought all its genius to bear on the task of superimposing huge blocks of basalt one on top of the other. Now that the evening sun bathed the walls with its ray of death, and the moonless night licked them, unable to suppress their wild boasting, Fartamio Andra do Nguélo Ndalo smoked her pipe and remarked that stones had always been man's best allies. The moon turned them silver and gave them eyes full of shadows. Each evening, their angles were thrown into a mild panic, like the sea when it's waiting for a storm. Transoms, archivolts, arches, pillars, volutes, bas reliefs, triforiums, turrets, foliated scrolls, dovetails, pylons, porticos, peristyles, monopteroi, lanterns, dungeons, all danced in the glow from the south, at the hour when the tropics give off their hard, graveyard smell. It was so beautiful that no one knew any more how to bring the building to an end.

When at last we thought the citadel was finished, Sarngata Nola ordered the construction of seven belfries – three facing Nsanga-Norda, two facing Valtano, one facing the sea, and one facing the lake. We sent for the Togolese sculptor, Paul Ahyi, to put eyes on the seventy Mexican candles on the tops of the pylons on the Nsanga-Norda side.

Then, from the four corners of the globe, journalists, film-makers, scholars and scientists began to arrive, as well as researchers with all kinds of reputations and all kinds of projects in mind, photographers, and the simply curious. They came by sea, by air and via Nsanga-Norda. We found we'd erected the most visited and the most photographed monument in the world. One night, Fartamio Andra and countless others even caught sight of a column of flying saucers circling our citadel. Estina Bronzario decided to celebrate the centenary we'd had to abandon the day Lorsa Lopez forced us to eat his crime instead, because she thought the flying saucers came from Nsanga-Norda.

'What a marvellous idea this was of Sarngata Nola's! He's turned stones into cash!'

'He's transformed the Coast into a paradise. We don't even need their capital any more.'

Lorsa Manuel Yeba organised binges. The Reverend Father Roguerio said masses. The puppet Lorsa Lopez ran about the town with thorns stuck in his nose, and the Beauty of Beauties, dressed in white, spent her days watching the sea. We'd all forgotten that Estina Bronzario was going to be killed, and that the police were due to come from the capital to investigate the crimes. Only the mayor and the judge did their utmost to preserve the evidence of the crimes. We danced and we ate. We danced and we ate, until the day when Mr 7 came to us and said: 'It's a magnificent shack you've put up here. I'd rather like to make it my palace.'

Mr 7's plans were reported to Sarngata Nola and Estina Bronzario.

'Over our dead bodies,' said Sarngata Nola.

'I'd rather see it turned into a brothel,' said Estina Bronzario. She dictated the following letter to Fartamio:

Honourable Mr 7,

I don't know if you deserve hate or respect. But I swear to you on my honour that it would be better for you to throw your idea of turning our citadel into a palace into the deepest hole you can find. We built it with our blood and our sweat. We shall defend it in the same way if we have to.

Yours faithfully,

Estina Bronzario

On the day we were at last to celebrate the centenary, the Beauty of Beauties painted her face white with kaolin and announced throughout the town that she was going to tell her secret in Estina Benta Square. Estina Bronzario said she wouldn't be going to hear the silly nonsense of the woman dressed in the stupid white of Nsanga-Norda.

A huge podium and three microphones were installed at the far end of the concourse. The crowd settled themselves under the trees and waited. The mayor and the judge came, not to hear the secret, but to make sure nothing was said against them. The crowd cheered Zarcanio Nala, the Beauty of Beauties, when she mounted the steps of the podium, went up to the microphones, cleared her throat and began to intone the shame and the name of the man who'd originally passed on the Nsanga-Norda lice. She sang to us how and from whom the man who'd originally passed on the lice had acquired them, how, when and where he'd passed the same filthy creatures on to her – alas! – as well, how he'd abandoned her with a child in her guts, in order to chase after a certain singer from the conservatoire. She danced the rumpus of shame, pronouncing the man's name several times as she did so, and then sang the piece of pieces, which we took up with tears in our eyes. No one dared leave Estina Benta Square.

Came the hour when the late Armano Yozua used to call the faithful to the afternoon prayer. We heard his voice and thought of the Valtano flies keeping watch over his body. And even though our reason told us that we'd only imagined hearing it, in our hearts we thought it really

97

was Armano Yozua's voice. We turned towards Baltayonsa. The man-woman was climbing the stairs to call the faithful.

The man who'd originally passed on the lice turned out to be my man, Paolo Cerbante. Yet his baptism of shame didn't upset me too much. I knew myself, and this was no normal situation. I'd always considered myself a champion of exclusivity in affairs of the heart, which I'd always regarded as a question of honour. I can share anything, absolutely anything, with anyone. But not my men! Anna Maria did once tell me, though, that my man had an odd way of looking at Estina Benta.

'The colours of desire deceive no one.'

'You must be making a mistake, Anna Maria,' Nelanda had said. 'Paolo Cerbante doesn't fool about among the petticoats.'

'All men are the same, sister. Whether they say it aloud or in a whisper, they love all beautiful women.'

'They do indeed, sister!'

Sometimes we react to the truth as if we were capable of murdering it. We stick the whole blade of our powerlessness into it. But it shows us its teeth and its transparence. We act as if we were able to negotiate our destiny. In fact, neither time nor truth belong to us. We have to realise that, at the end of the day, we're alone in the world. The great reality of man is his infinite solitude, which lasts right up to the day he dies. That was how my thinking went the day my man was covered with shame.

At the moment when, tearing her white dress as a sign of Paolo Cerbante's dishonour, the Beauty of Beauties left the podium, we heard someone shouting and we all turned round to face the direction of Nsanga-Norda. We saw Fartamio Andra coming from the bayou, her cloth flung over her left shoulder and carrying her slippers in her hand, without the glasses she always wore because of her long-sightedness, and without her long ebony stick carved by the founders of our town. She was shouting and weeping in all the languages of the Coast: 'Estina Bronzario's been killed! What a disaster!' As at the time of Estina Benta's murder, everyone crossed themselves as Fartamio Andra passed. 'God! What a disaster! They've killed her!'

Around three-thirty in the afternoon, under a velvet sky, a huge crowd gathered on the stones of the bayou, trampling the ground like a herd of cattle, stamping their feet, growling and seething. All the faces were swimming in sorrow, overcome by impotence and shame. By anger, too. But by that anger which has no clear object and comes over you when you have it in for God as well. Mother!

Nothing, apart from her fichu, her crinoline in shreds, and her medals laid out on the fichu, under her madras, nothing indicated that this was indeed Estina Bronzario's body. It had been cut up into pieces. Her heart had been placed on the fichu with her medals, where it continued to beat. Next to the fichu, three words were written in lipstick on a scrap of petticoat: 'Wait for the police.' Her two pegs and her two shoulders lay on a huge log left behind by the high waters of March and April. On the sand, inundated with flies and nibbled by red ants, were her still-smoking intestines. Nearby, her flayed, eyeless head laughed a ghostly laugh. Her stomach had been opened up and emptied of its contents. They, too, were still smoking: beans, pimentos, sticks of yam, vegetables, fish, all the nosh from the centenary banned by the authorities. Ants were parading all over them; flies, too. We saw Nertez Coma standing looking down at them. He was holding three rainbow perch strung together with a liana cord, which went in through the mouth and came out again through the gills. The man was weeping silently.

'To make sure they don't accuse him,' said Fartamio do Nguélo Ndalo.

As on the day of the ceremony of the shaming and unmarrying, all eyes were turned on him. His hands were spotless.

'A shame on us if we can't stop all this madness,' shouted Nertez Coma, before bursting into sobs as heavy as the waters that batter the Coast below the cliff.

Everyone began to sob along with Nertez Coma. Hard, hot tears of impotence and hate. In everyone's eyes. In the women's eyes, in the men's eyes, in the children's eyes, all gazing on this harsh wickedness, on this harsh shame of man spread out on the agate stones, on this stomach of man tipped over the proud brambles of his barbarity: the absolute ugliness of our vanity. A salt without taste!

Our noses drank in the new odour of our sister Estina Bronzario (if she it was), the harsh odour of the blood of the Coast, the harsh odour of flesh mingling with the odours of the evening wind. The coarse odour of man caught in the trap of hate. The odour of the butcher's knife that has cut off the metaphysical breath of the Coast, its hope, its dream and its right.

'What are we doing?' asked the judge.

'You know very well we're waiting for the police,' replied the mayor. 'Tell Nertez Coma to photograph the pieces and send us the invoice.'

'*Esa mierda*,' sighed Artamio de la Casa.

'*Cavadonsé*,' said the judge, thinking he was in Nsanga-Norda.

Nertez Coma went to fetch his equipment and returned to photograph the body of Estina Bronzario, without charge. As a precaution, the mayor had the location of each of the parts left whole marked with paint: pegs, shoulders, head, torso, neck, pelvis. Nertez Coma was also asked to photograph the multitude. Sarngata Nola tore up his purple poncho and put on Nsanga-Norda blue. He told his actors to dance the rumpus of mourning, to tear their crinolines into rags and throw some of the rags beside the body of Estina Bronzario (if she it was), and to proclaim the ruin and shame of Nsanga-Norda. Zarcanio Nala intoned the hymn of the Coast. No one left the bayou until three in the morning. The mayor and the judge went to change, but came back very quickly.

From the next day on, the mayor sent three telegrams a day to the authorities: one at a quarter past seven, one at eleven o'clock, and one at four o'clock. To prevent the ants from nibbling the body, Lorsa Manuel Yeba poured cresyl mixed with Nsanga-Norda bird-lime over it. Maniana Cuenso and the theosophist, Larkansa, brought oils to delay putrefaction. As we were worried about the rains, Anna Maria took a live toad and ground it in a mortar with ashes and soil from the cemetery. Fartamio Andra do Nguélo Ndalo added quicklime and palm twigs. 'There's nothing for wetting here,' sang the women.

We wondered who was going to be killed after Estina Bronzario. Some thought it would be Sarngata Nola. Others, Fartamio Andra. Two years after Estina Bronzario's death, the mayor was still sending his three daily telegrams to the authorities, with no sign of a decision on their part to send the police. We made love, danced all the rumpuses, encircled by our cowardice and our powerlessness to say who was going to be killed before whom. But we were no longer afraid. As Fartamio Andra do Nguélo Ndalo liked to tell us, we'd left fear fifty years behind us. We were about to kill death itself.

'*Esa mierda*,' said Nertez Coma, the day we found, alongside the pieces of Estina Bronzario still waiting by the bayou for the police, the Beauty of Beauties' costume, covered in blood with, next to that horror, these words: 'Nsanga-Norda is not the bastion of stupidity.'

No one could make any sense of it all. Nansa Mopata tried to explain it by preaching that Estina Bronzario's death and Fr Bona of the Sacristy's disappearance were connected, but this was too incredible, and no one paid any attention to her prophecies of doom. The only thing that didn't leave the multitudes indifferent was the presence, next to the Beauty of Beauties' costume, of a gigantic portrait of the Supreme Consul of Nsanga-Norda in ceremonial dress, with these words scribbled on the top of his kepi crowned with seven *kamichi* feathers: 'Your heart is one with mine in the universal heart of things.'

Later, Lorsa Manuel Yeba, the thrower of binges, concocted the following story on the basis of judicious hypotheses: the consul had been in love with the Beauty of Beauties, who was herself in love with my man.

'You'll get into trouble with the authorities if you go on telling that story of yours,' Machedo Palma said to him.

'They've never done anything to you, and you're always criticising the authorities.'

'That's not the point. The authorities love people to say things about them, good or bad, the way I do it. It amuses them, it's all part of the democracy game. But in your case, you're too close to the truth. And take my word for it, truth isn't part of the democracy game.'

'*Esa mierda*,' said the judge, passing his eating hand over his big crocodile's jaw.

'*Grosso mierda*,' said the mayor.

A telegram had come from Nsanga-Norda. Six words in all: 'Bury Estina Bronzario. Stop and end.' The mayor, who was frightened of losing his job, gave orders for the funeral to take place. But Sarngata Nola announced that he wasn't going to let Estina Bronzario be buried like a dog.

'If there are men in this town, let them prepare to get it up. The crime may be over, but hate goes on.'

He seized the three small trench mortars belonging to the eight border guards based on the Island of Solitudes, repaired the Big Bertha abandoned at the entrance to the tunnel by the troops who guarded the Nsanga-Norda railway line, and shut himself in the citadel with forty pygmies and six Valancia men, including Lorsa Manuel Yeba, the thrower of binges, Elmunto Yema, the station-master, Machedo Palma, the man who'd always criticised the authorities, and our sister, Sonia O. Almeida.

That same day, at four o'clock in the afternoon, the police arrived from Nsanga-Norda accompanied by the federal medical officer, Artanso Paolo Nola, and the federal judge, Roano Giovano Landra. There were ninety-six of them altogether. We couldn't understand why they sang the *Magnificat* instead of the national anthem or the song of Nsanga-Norda. Nor could we understand why, instead of their official uniforms, they sported the great gown of the Coast surmounted by the star of Nsanga-Norda and, on their left shoulder, the purple velvet chaperon. They made their way to the town square, where the mayor had finished reconstituting the murder scene, with his odd habit of adding his own glasses, his slippers and the judge's chaperon to the other objects connected with the crime. But instead of stopping, they made their way towards the new quarter of Huenda-Norda, where a few months after Estina Bronzario's murder, Estando Douma had built a brothel thirty-five storeys high to show off the money his screwing machines had made from the misfortune of others. The brothel's chief customers weren't Valancians but tourists who came to see the citadel, or the growing numbers of whites who were hunting the brontosaurus and the atlantosaurus in the Devil's tidal reservoirs on the other side of the cliff, which hadn't stopped bawling since Estina Bronzario's death.

As for Huenda-Norda, it had no school, no dispensary, no market, no theatre, only two grandiose monstrosities, the brothel and the pub. These two horrors belonged to the same Estando Douma everyone called 'the devil's father-in-law'. The brothel received half a million piss merchants every two weeks, the pub had a turnover of seven million bottles of beer a day. The other function of the brothel was to serve at one and the same time as school, dispensary and market. Huenda-Norda, phoney paradise of glass, smelt of milt and pee. The only truly happy princes were the mosquitoes and the toads. Everything else was phoney: phoney men, phoney promenaders, phoney lovers, phoney rich, phoney thinkers, phoney VIPs, phoney aristocrats, phoney human beings.

'Estina Bronzario would never have allowed this monstrosity two steps from her bayou. All those poor women with their wooden arses, nailed to the shame of having to piss money, nailed to the absurdity of having to piss their daily bread. They may all be from Nsanga-Norda, but even so Estina Bronzario would never have allowed it.'

The police, the medical officer and the federal judge took their siesta while we waited for them in the town square. After their siesta, they went to have a drink at Elmano Zola's widow's place. They only arrived at the scene of the crime when the sun, tired of waiting for them, was putting on its night-dress and preparing to plunge into its bed of flaming islands over by Afonso. The judge gave the officer in charge of the police the photos of the crimes taken by Nertez Coma. He looked at the photos and smiled, a long smile full of malice.

'Judge, have the photographer locked up.'

'What?' asked the judge, in surprise.

'I may be a little drunk' (he reeked of wine), 'but these photos have been falsified. I can't find that chaperon or those slippers at the scene of the crime.'

The judge tried to explain, but the police officer told him to arrest Nertez Coma in the name of the law. Just as the police were putting the handcuffs on to the wrists of the ex-municipal photographer, we heard a muffled explosion from the direction of Huenda-Norda. As the earth shook under us, we couldn't help thinking of the cliff's cry.

'We're encircled by destiny,' said Manuel Coma. 'I still haven't registered that Estina Bronzario has really gone, any more than I can accept this idiotic arrival of the police. They should've stayed in Nsanga-Norda. We were quite used to our despair. We'd become attached to our misfortune. What difference can they make to our slump into the void?'

Manuel Coma shouted at the top of his voice that he didn't care a damn about the police, that he didn't care a damn about the authorities or their investigations, that our country was nothing but a terrible, empty slogan. He tore up his clothes and went off in the direction of the Island of Solitudes, where Lorsa Lopez still barked, haunted by the demons of his crime.

We were to learn, late that night, that the thirty-five storeys of Estando Douma's brothel had been blown up and the whole place turned into an inferno by the explosion we'd heard. The police wouldn't allow anyone to go home. When they'd completed their inquiries concerning Estina Benta's murder, we all trooped round to Elmano Zola's place. The officer in charge took Fr Bona's prayer book from the freezer where Elmano Zola was sleeping his death and bleeding as if he'd only been killed the day before.

'When did you kill him?' the officer in charge asked the judge.

'Forty-seven years ago,' said the mayor.

We went to the bayou for Estina Bronzario. We knew that Sarngata Nola and his rebels had removed the pieces of her body. The night was cold, but the officer in charge was determined to complete his investigations by daybreak. We went to the Nsanga-Norda road for Salmano Ruenta, and finally to Baltayonsa, where the flies still kept watch day and night over the muezzin's body. After that, the tribunal arrived from Nsanga-Norda, composed of police and magistrates, dressed as Sarngata Nola's actors had been the day they came from the capital. To our great surprise, Fartamio Andra informed us that the court was going to try Lorsa Lopez's parrot.

'For spreading the rumour about the lap lice and thus obliging Lorsa Lopez to commit his crime,' said Sonia O. Almeida.

'Ah! Those Nsanga-Nordans, they've got their capacity for closing their eyes down to a fine art,' said Anna Maria.

The parrot was sent for. It was dressed in the colours of the Coast. This didn't please Fartamio Andra, who wrote and sent to the Palace of Arts and Crafts, where the court was sitting, the following letter of protest:

Dear Gentlemen of the Court,

The Coast acknowledges your right to try the parrot for any crime you wish, and to pass judgement on it in your own good time. The Coast will allow you to dispense justice as you see fit and as you please. But so long as there remains a single man or woman whose placenta has been thrown into

104

the ditch of honour at Yoltana, the Coast will retain its ancient practice of pissing on anything that runs counter to its honour or its dignity. As the mouthpiece of the Coast, I ask you to respect the colours of its dignity.

Fartamio Andra

She received a reply to the effect that the authorities had decided the matter and that the court was not competent to change what the authorities had ordained.

So the parrot kept the colours of the Coast. From his retreat, Sarngata Nola heard what had happened, and threatened to liquidate the members of the court if the colours of Valancia were not respected.

The podium of the court had been erected opposite the parrot's cage. It was richly decorated. It had also been decided (by the authorities, it was said) that the bird would be tried on a Thursday, the day when the deceased woman had been killed by her man. During the two days that preceded the trial, the town square was occupied by three or four thousand armed soldiers, brought in to guard the Coast and protect the court. In spite of the provocation of the crowds hurling abuse at them, in spite of being harassed by mosquitoes and children, the soldiers never flinched. Hardly batting an eyelid, they seemed made of stone in their champagne-coloured uniforms, and their motionless pop-guns seemed to look on with amusement at the hordes of kids pelting these men of death with Nsanga-Norda apples. Then, what the Valancians called the Day of the Parrot finally arrived. More than eight thousand souls surrounded the town square. The multitudes stretched as far as the Bayou and the Tourniquet quarters on the Nsanga-Norda side, and Huenda-Norda on the lake side.

'I've never seen so many people,' said Fartamio Andra.

'They've come from all over the Coast,' said Anna Maria.

'The Coast and the islands,' corrected Fartamio Andra do Nguélo Ndalo.

The sixteen arquebus shots announcing the start of the trial were fired. The president of the court called for silence. A deathly hush fell on the crowd. Then Lorsa Lopez appeared, wearing the same colours as his parrot. He went up to the president and addressed him in these terms: 'I've come to answer for my crime. Because I was born in honour and dignity, but especially because I don't have the Nsanga-Nordans' heart. I don't have their bird-lime flesh. I don't have their salamander soul. I came into the world for honour. I've remained in it for honour. Here I am.'

But the president ordered the officers of the court to remove 'this madman who seems to be ignorant of the fact that the affairs of this world do not concern madmen.'

'I killed her,' Lorsa Lopez went on, 'because at four forty-five that day I returned home from the town hall, where we'd been doing everything we could to prevent Estina Bronzario from celebrating the banned centenary, and found her in my bed, in the arms of . . .'

'Take him away,' thundered the president of the court.

A dozen soldiers swooped down on Lorsa Lopez, who disappeared in a metallic welter of seething uniforms, like a cricket in a nest of red ants. We felt sorry for him. He re-emerged at the other end of the tornado of green berets, torn and bleeding like a skinned doe, as naked as he was when his mother brought him into the world.

'Valancia has become a heartless place,' sighed Fartamio Andra.

And we turned our gaze on Colbado, with its jumble of streets which sometimes finished up in a marsh, its stinking refuse, its faeces, its dead animals and its foul water, while the court of the Nsanga-Norda fools set about cross-examining Lorsa Lopez's bird. The parrot's only reply to all the questions was: 'Lice. She gave him lice.'

'Comrade Parrot, try and show a little imagination. How do you know that the lice didn't come from Lorsa Lopez?' asked the judge-general from Nsanga-Norda.

'You're a fool!' screamed the parrot.

The judge banged the table. His eyes became red with anger. Words choked in his throat, constricted by hate and fury. He got up from his seat and walked about for some time in an effort to control his anger. He told the court cooks to bring him some coffee. The coffee was slow in coming. The judge went up to the parrot and, by way of filling in time while he waited for his coffee, he asked another question:

'In your opinion, who gave the lice to Madame Lorsa Lopez?'

The parrot laughed out loud, to everyone's surprise. It sang the hymn of the Seven Solitudes composed by Lorsa Lopez:

106

I am the pure and simple
Child of a woman
From one end to the other of my life
I am the pure and simple
Piece of a woman
From one end to the other of myself
I have prided myself
In the pure and simple desire
To name the earth day and night.

'It was you,' said the parrot.

The judge spat on the parrot. We took it that he was spitting on the colours of the Coast. The crowd rose to its feet in a body and dispersed, shouting its anger and disappointment. Then it made its way to the citadel where Sarngata Nola and his rebels were guarding Estina Bronzario's remains. No one had ever seen such a dense crowd in Valancia, a crowd driven by hate and anger and armed with fishermen's and builders' tools.

'You'll soon find out, Judge, that no one insults the Coast!'

The green men from Nsanga-Norda were left on their own in the town square, still as motionless as the muzzles of their pop-guns, while an angry mass of new faces danced around the citadel, singing (it's not quite clear why) the hymn of the Seven Solitudes. Then, when the crowd was at the foot of the citadel, Larmanso Kongo called out as follows to Sarngata Nola: 'Nsanga-Norda has just insulted the Coast. We are joining with you to avenge our shame.'

The crowd sat down to await Sarngata Nola's reply, for among us there are words which can only be listened to in that position.

In the distance, over by the island, the sea also seemed to sit down to await Valancia's reply to Nsanga-Norda. Space entered into communion with the crowds. Sarngata Nola appeared on top of a turret on the north side of the citadel. He went up to the pylons which completed the citadel to the left of those who had their backs to the sea, and raised his arms to greet the crowd.

There was an explosion of lungs and mouths that shook the sky above our heads. At least that was our impression. Sarngata Nola was wearing the same mourning surcoat he'd put on the day Estina

Bronzario was massacred. The citadel had been built on a sort of huge cone formed by the menhirs left by the seven kings, on the outskirts of the Bayou quarter where Estina Bronzario's house was. We knew that the stones for the house had been provided by the twelfth Founders Line and that it was between three and four centuries old. Even though the citadel itself was only nine years old, its fearsome walls and buttresses had been devoured by the ivy, stinging nettles and goose-berries of the prophet Mouzediba. The salt had turned them grey in places. Thousands of flying foxes, vampire bats, thrushes, humming-birds, cockatoos and Valancia birds were nesting in its gargoyles and multi-shaped curves. On its southern side lived colonies of chattering monkeys.

'The musician-monkeys descend from men,' said Fartamio Andra do Nguélo Ndalo.

Sarngata Nola opened his mouth to say things the multitude was not expecting to hear.

'Honour forbids us to shed Nsanga-Norda blood. We'll only fight if they attack us. And only when they've killed ten thousand seven hundred and twelve of us.'

The fury of the crowd turned to bitterness. Pitchforks, fishermen's knives, spades, shovels, picks and machetes were all deposited at the foot of the citadel, to await the day when Nsanga-Norda would have killed ten thousand seven hundred and twelve of us.

'What about the shame?' asked Larmanso Kongo of him who, we now knew, was to be the new soul of our metaphysical land.

'They've spat on our colours, but not in our hearts,' said Sarngata Nola. 'So long as his heart hasn't been sullied, a man remains pure.'

'What about Estina Bronzario's death?' asked Anna Maria.

There was a deep silence. The crowd waited. But Sarngata Nola didn't speak.

Then we heard the Mahometan of Baltayonsa calling out. Artamio de la Casa came to tell us that the parrot had been shot for abuse of confidence, falsehood and practice of falsehood, and that, as he gave up his fine multicoloured soul, the creature had revealed the name of the man who'd originally passed on the lice as that of Armano Yozua, who'd got them from the wife of the Secateur of Nsanga-Norda, who had herself acquired them from the Procurator of Nsanga-Norda.

'What a sickening business!' sighed Fartamio Andra do Nguélo Ndalo.

'There is now no need for us to kill anyone,' Sarngata Nola continued to declare five months after the day the parrot was shot in the town square by the soldiers from Nsanga-Norda. 'Shedding the blood of others is senseless. Love is the exact science of human life. But, comrades, we'd be foolish to fold our arms while the rest of the world advances. We've mourned Estina Bronzario long enough. The Coast isn't a kindergarten! The Coast is not, and never will be, a land of little people. We've said as much to those impertinent Nsanga-Nordans. Now, comrades, let us say it to ourselves: Estina Bronzario is dead, but life goes on, for her and for us. Let all of you who agree with me, all of you who are volunteers for life and progress, for honour and dignity, from now on wear this badge.'

He held up the star of solidarity for the crowd to see. For, during their retreat, Sarngata Nola's rebels had not been making weapons as we'd thought, but these badges. Dressed in purple and white, they now came out of the citadel carrying large baskets, to distribute stars of solidarity to any who wanted them.

'We're all cripples,' said Anna Maria, when she saw Sarngata Nola distributing the little bronze crosses surmounted with the star of Nsanga-Norda. 'We won't ever know who killed Estina Bronzario.'

She broke a piece of kola and gave it to the man who was offering her a solidarity volunteer's badge. Lorsa Manuel Yeba took the kola and smiled before chewing it.

'We're caught in the trap of Estina Bronzario's flesh. We are, all of us, marked with the stupid flesh of Estina Bronzario. How could it be otherwise? Whatever anyone says, love is still the one true absolute of life. All the ways were closed. One remained open behind us, only one: death. And since we didn't want to die, we chose life.'

'It was Estina Bronzario herself who came to tell Sarngata Nola to change the war,' muttered Machedo Palma. 'You may not be able to believe me, but we all saw her, and we laid down our arms to make the stars. Bronzario was accompanied by the Beauty of Beauties, and they were singing the piece of pieces. It was an incredible vision. She was wearing the gown of Nsanga-Norda, while the Beauty of Beauties was dressed in the colours of the Coast. Mother, if only you could have seen it! And when Bronzario saw the pieces of her body, she laughed these words: "Sarngata Nola, the body of death has departed; here is the body of life. I invite you to know that hate is over." "But, Estina Bronzario, all of us here only have the body of hate left." And, as we all turned at the same moment towards the cliff, we saw the Virgin of Solitudes, just as the Founders Line had described her to us after they saw her in 777 BC, above the Island of Solitudes, holding in her left hand the purple flame, the symbol of the inhabitants of Eldouranta, and in her right hand the secretary bird and the merino sheep of Nsanga-Norda. "Today is really the day Estina Benta should have died," the Virgin said, and we all heard her. But when we turned round again and looked for Estina Bronzario, we saw no one.'

The other thing carried by the Virgin, according to Machedo Palma's account, was the parrot, dressed in the colours of the Coast and, as on the day when it was shot, singing the poem of the Seven Solitudes. But the narrator was unable to tell us what the small creature was that slept at the feet of the Virgin.

'It was a sable or a Valtano serval.'

Just as he was unable to say for sure whether the bird was a parrot, a wood-pigeon or a quetzal.

'Whatever it was, it sang the hymn of the Solitudes,' said Machedo Palma.

'The poem of the Seven Solitudes,' corrected one of Sarngata Nola's pygmies.

'The Virgin was carried on a quadriga which floated in the air.' (No one could swallow this, even if it was the Virgin.)

Machedo Palma's narrative was confirmed by Sarngata Nola, who acknowledged the facts with a nod of his head. He continued to distribute the peace volunteer badges, while listening to the oath bequeathed by the woman of bronze: 'On my honour and on my life, I shall not take up arms against Nsanga-Norda until the day when they have massacred ten thousand seven hundred and twelve children of the Coast. Then will come the day of the parrot, the day when the sky and the earth will be joined together.'

110

5

Nsanga-Norda

Every sleep has its awakening. I'll go and see Aunt Mangala. She'll give me the money for the ticket, with a little advice thrown in: 'It's good when a woman shows courage; she's truer to herself then than when she's happy.'

She always speaks like this. And I'll agree with her. She'll offer me a piece of smoked pipe-fish. I'll eat it to please her. But when I tell her that because of my solitude I must leave Valancia for Nsanga-Norda, she'll throw a fit. 'I'd rather see you go to your grave. You have the seven tattoos of Estina Bronzario. How can you choose shame? We're waiting for the day when Nsanga-Norda kills ten thousand seven hundred and twelve of us. Then the sky and the earth will be joined together. Nsanga-Norda's a heartless place. It's the capital of vanity. No child of the Coast can trail her soul about that dump.'

We'll look one another in the eye for a long moment. Then she'll speak of my husband. Aunt Mangala has never liked Paolo Cerbante. It was because of him that she left Estina Bronzario's house to go and live in the Tourniquet quarter.

'He smells like a rat and I can't stand it. He'd be better living in a hole, smelling like that. Like a rotting lote.'

'It's the smell of the male,' laughed Fartamio Andra do Nguélo Ndalo. 'The strong smell that kills the female.'

'It's the smell of the demon,' explained Lorsa Manuel Yeba. 'Apparently they pass it on from father to son in Nsanga-Norda.'

But I wanted to be the wife of the man who smelt like the devil. Fr Bona married us before the Coast and before God. The Coast didn't understand. How could Estina Bronzario's granddaughter marry a vulture? She prattled on, but love, all love, is nothing if not a scandal. The heart that loves is answerable only to the logic of love. I loved Paolo Cerbante.

111

Aunt Mangala will say what she's always said, since the day the Coast first found out that my man was sleeping with Helen. 'Philosophy is the science of the sick, I agree. Since we're all sick in this sick world, we'll always need a little philosophy. When your man decides to sleep around, it's hard to take. But believe me, Gracia, in this jungle of cocks and cunts, we each have to try and cope with our own solitude as best we can. You'll tell me that these are just words and that life is more real than words. That you have nothing left when you lose your heart. But you're young, you can find another man and perhaps he'll be an *hombre de honor*. You'll begin again. The earth, the cliff, the sand, the wind ... The metaphysical Coast! This was how our ancestors wanted it. We aren't like those gutless Nsanga-Nordans. Some lands can only produce turds of bronze. Others, alas, can only manage men who can't see further than their noses.'

She'll talk all night, eating pimento like her sister Estina Bronzario, who believed that pimento keeps women young. But I'll take the train to Nsanga-Norda. I hope the Coast will forgive me. We've asked too much of it. We've made it hard. We've created a monster. We've used its stones to make our ribs. We've tried to change its stones into hearts. Just as we knew Lorsa Lopez was going to kill his wife and that Estina Bronzario was going to be slaughtered, we know, too, that one day the Coast will die, eaten by the sea. What can we do about it? Time is our enemy.

Since Estina Bronzario's death, Fartamio Andra hasn't been able to control the trembling of her hands. Her body has gone into decline. Her sight has deteriorated, her heart has evaporated with her memory. Her vigour has dried up. Poor Fartamio Andra.

'You really mean to go to that town?'

'Yes.'

'Estina Bronzario wouldn't have forgiven you. No child of the Coast can walk on a soil that's a hundred times cursed.'

'It's my destiny. I won't try and avoid it.'

My man has come. Neither Fartamio Andra nor even Fartamio Andra do Nguélo Ndalo has spoken to him. He threw himself into an armchair. His eyes are closed but his eyelids are watching. Anna Maria offers him some tea. She knows his tastes: wines, colours, food ... While he drinks his tea, he looks at the portrait of Estina Bronzario painted by Sarngata Nola to fill the emptiness that Estina Bronzario's absence has brought into this house. I think of our room. In this house inhabited by so many mysteries since the second Founders Line. The strong odour of the female bathes my loins. We come into the world to name: let whoever names their perdition or their shame beware. I think of the time when he and I were us. Of the ardour of our skins. Of the breath of love. Of the taste of the air. Of the magnificent odour of the world clinging tightly to things. Of the flesh of two people alight with the fire of a common madness, resting on a common hope. Awkwardly. And of time licking the whole.

'Will you let me explain, Gracia?'

'If it's to tell me you're sleeping with Helen, I know that already. I saw you on the night of the carnival, at Mateyonsa.'

The odour of the female becomes fragrance of lemon. The weight of the body dissolves in the giddiness of my woman's outraged vanity. He doesn't say anything. He's looking at a fashion magazine. Paris in summer. Paris beneath the tropics. I was very beautiful then: bronze, slender, with a model's neck and a mouth as round as the world. In love, I wasn't yet the dead wood I've become, but fire, as we say, voracious, insatiable. Inflammable. We saw a doctor to moderate my voracity for things of the flesh. A Valtano traditional doctor ordered me not to eat hot food but to taste the flesh of the *umbra*. We sought the advice of friends who, in turn, sought advice on our behalf. 'She should marry Estando Douma,' was Fernando Lambert's suggestion. Things changed when Nansa advised me to sit every morning and every evening over an infusion of cajuput. 'Thanks to this treatment, Marcellio Douma's wife has stopped sleeping around like a bitch on heat. Now they're happy together.'

'I can't expect you to eat a dead woman. I know you like fire. A great bush fire that eats everything. My blood could do just that once: speak fire. Alas! I gorged myself. I used up my woman's assets, and I also used up my share of the world at the same time.'

'I'd thought at first of killing Paolo Cerbante. But killing's for fools. Killing's for cops.

'If you'll let me, Gracia, I can explain everything.'

I burst into tears. I don't want to cry in front of him. But the body always wins.

'There's nothing left between us, Paolo Cerbante! I want you to have no illusions about that.'

Helen's dead. And it's me he comes for. While he waits for a new Helen!

> You are for my eyes
> This world dressed up
> That always awaits
> My soul and my teeth.

I see our footsteps, again, in the sand's memory. God! When is love not madness? I hear our lovemaking again, beneath the noise of the waves. All the winds are marked by it. Water's still what we have best in the world. It has filled itself with waves and mist. It's a girl carrying the heavy tear of her deflowering. Over there, out at sea, softly, the Island of Solitudes says the *Our Father*. Die? No! My own death must do justice to the tricks life has played on me. The fields of Sarngata Nola fix me with their eyes of maize and yellow cotton. I look at the hundred thousand crosses planted the whole length of the Coast, like silent sages. I feel myself two: the self that speaks and the self that replies.

'My husband was an exceptional man.'

'Open your eyes, Gracia!'

'My body's still greedy for this world.'

'Gracia,' Fartamio Andra says to me. 'Nsanga-Norda has no soul. You can go tomorrow if you still want to.'

'Tomorrow's not our day, Fartamio Andra. Tomorrow belongs only to tomorrow.'

He throws himself in front of me, almost shouting.

'My love! The meaning of my life! I'll kill myself if you leave. Stay! I can explain everything, absolutely everything. I'm to blame. It's my fault. My sin. And my shame.'

He doesn't realise that we have reached the point of no return. For me, it must be said, the vagina is a temple. You come to it to worship honour and the sublime simplicity of the body. My own body can't accept that Helen died in order to lay claim to his passion. Goodbye, Valancia. I'll go and dry my shame in Nsanga-Norda.

While Aunt Mangala prepares a piece of pipe-fish for my breakfast,

114

the telephone rings. She lifts the receiver. Her old eyes tremble. She frowns.

'Who is it?'

'Him.'

'Ring off!'

'He says it's important.'

'Ring off.'

It was here that we met. I'd come, partly, to take stock. I was at university at the time. I wanted to talk a different language from that of the chopped, bombarded, kneaded, welded, heartless, fleshless atom. I dropped out of my studies to give myself time to love him. I regret nothing. I had the chance to be happy, with that stupid joy that comes to us from the womb. The cult of the body. When it's all fire. I listened to the song of the grain of sand as it celebrates its entry into the waves. The fleshy corolla opening its heart, drying its soul in the sun. The evening wind that extinguishes everything, one by one. The fragrant waters of the Rouvièra Verda in which Estina Bronzario must have washed her body before she was massacred and thrown on to the stones. The waters of the sea, bellowing over by Afonso. The great, fractured dream of the stones of Baltayonsa. Colonnades. Menhirs. Under our dazzled sky, which always forgets to let go of the sun in the evening. Love can only do two things: save or kill.

I ate the pipe-fish. It was very good. Then, because I was so tired, I slept with my head on the table. Aunt Mangala watched over me all through the night. I don't think much of her – she comes up with ideas I don't like. When you make her angry, she's capable of throwing her cigarette in your face, whoever you are! That's probably why she's burnt down six homes and lives alone with her cat and her parrot. Her neighbours often come round for a meal. Old da Souza also comes to eat with her. And when she has to eat elsewhere, Aunt Mangala always takes her animals with her. The cat weighs eleven kilos and eats like a husband. The parrot is incredibly stupid, but it's good at killing bad silences.

'I haven't been able to go out since that mad neighbour of mine, Dongala, came and took my cat to cook and eat it.'

Fortunately, the cat put up a fight. She was lucky it didn't scratch out those conger eel eyes of hers.

115

Me, thunder. Me, torrid. Extinguished. Dead. Finished. Me, fury! Me! If only I could have gone into Estando Douma's brothels. You open your legs to the first comer. For as long as he needs to shoot his load. You spit. You go and wash yourself. This time, it's a water without anguish. Water pure and simple. A tic, just like the mayor's ears that made Salmano Ruenta laugh. The spittle rumpus.

There were about a hundred of us in the compartment and the train was travelling at full speed towards Nsanga-Norda. But, at the spot where Carlanzo Mana's tent once stood, the driver slowed down. Then the train stopped. Soldiers came on board. Like those who'd come for the investigations, they all wore the great gown with the star of Nsanga-Norda and the purple velvet chaperon.

'We're looking for Sarngata Nola. You've nothing to fear if you're not Sarngata Nola. We won't hurt you.'

'But everyone knows that Sarngata Nola's in Valancia, in his citadel,' said an old woman, who must have been from Nsanga-Norda but who, oddly, could pronounce the *b* as we of the Coast did.

The man in the gown ignored the old woman. His companions were carrying huge portraits of Sarngata Nola, which they held up to our faces to force us to look at them. They pulled beards and hair to check that they were real, and scratched people's faces to satisfy themselves they, too, were real. And since Sarngata Nola had never in all his life been able to say the word *engender* (he always said *engendrer*), they made us take turns pronouncing this word. Poor Mallata Riza, in her agitation, mispronounced the devil's word, so they made her say it over and over again. The other word that Sarngata Nola had never been able to pronounce properly was *police* (he said *poolice*). For hours on end, they made Mallata Riza say it over and over.

'Please repeat, Madame: *police.*'

'*Police*, sir!'

'Again!'

'*Police.*'

She was trembling with fright and sweating profusely. Her vast body began to smell like a woman being worked. Her eyes were rolling so much they gave the impression they wanted to get away.

'*Police.* Please repeat, Madame.'

'*Police*, sir!'

'Again!'

'You'll kill her if you go on like that!' exploded Paolo Cerbante, whom I noticed for the first time since our departure.

'Shut your gov, sir,' replied the policeman, without even looking at him.

'You're torturing her for nothing, anyway, since Sarngata Nola isn't a woman.'

'I'm telling you to velt up,' said the policeman. 'Police. Repeat, Madame.'

But Mallata Riza had passed out. The policeman tried in vain to revive her.

They made poor Bertani Zola, who'd eaten a hundred times at the Valancia fair, repeat Sarngata Nola's words for two weeks. We couldn't understand why the other word the actor hadn't ever been able to pronounce wasn't on the test list: Nsanga-Norda. We knew, and so did the authorities, that Sarngata Nola always said Nesanga-Norde.

'They tried to get Elmano Zola's corpse to say the word. She couldn't reach an agreement with the authorities in Valancia, so his widow was taking it to Nsanga-Norda, where he'd asked to be buried.'

'It's because they've been edgy since Sarngata Nola said he was going to bury Estina Bronzario's remains in Nsanga-Norda, isn't it, sister? They're frightened for their consciences!'

'Has Sarngata Nola gone mad?'

'Of course not, sister. Secret negotiations are taking place between him and the authorities. Don't we all know that politics is above all the science of successful entertainment? Sarngata Nola is going to be made mayor. That's what'll happen. You can cut off my hand if it doesn't.'

'It won't happen,' said the other old woman, who'd been talking relentlessly since the train's departure.

This woman, who was as fat as a rhinoceros, reeked of Valtano beer. Her teeth were as pink as the flag of Faranta Muerta. She had the evil eye of the people of Westina. She said she'd only come to Valancia to see Nertez Coma's shaming.

'No, I can't live on the Coast. They love death there. They're obsessed with dying young.'

117

At the exit to the tunnel, we came to a camp of men dressed like hog hunters. The camp, we were told, was celebrating its seventh anniversary. A group of militiamen swept some of the young girls off to dance.

The merrymakers filled the train with flowers, palms, and cloths of shimmering colours. We couldn't understand why we were the object of such a wild and delirious welcome. They kept firing their blunder-busses into the air, and served us dishes of *pleurotus* mushrooms and Nsanga-Norda *amanita* mushrooms, which is the greatest honour you can do a guest anywhere on the Coast. Bagpipes and xylophones coughed and neighed their melodious tunes. There was even a dish of swallows' nests cooked with aubergines. They sat us down in a shelter just by the entrance to the big tent. The whole camp was redolent of cooking smells and the fragrance of wines, like Valancia on the eve of the tragic Thursday when Lorsa Lopez was to kill Estina Benta. All that was missing was the lake, the cliff and muezzin Armano Yozua calling the faithful.

A mulatto couple were seated in the tent of honour, a few steps from the shelter where we were eating. The man was wearing a huge pectoral brooch, which glittered with a thousand fires and a thousand colours. His wife (if she was his wife) had the same looks as the Beauty of Beauties and her smile revealed large, round, brilliant white teeth. Then the couple began to sing the Nsanga-Nordan version of the *Magnificat*, with the strongly Mahometan features that the muezzin brotherhood had skilfully incorporated into it. While they sang, a heavy silence hung over the motionless crowd (as was always the case when the *Magnificat* was sung in Valancia or Nsanga-Norda; the only time the *Magnificat* was sung by people who moved was the day the police arrived).

'It was at this time of the day that Nsanga-Norda was eaten by the waters,' a militiawoman explained to us when the couple had finished their performance.

'Nsanga-Norda or the Island of Eldouranta?' asked the fat woman, continuing to stuff herself with swallows' nests.

'Nsanga-Norda, sister. Just look on your left and you'll see for yourself. Isn't it incredible? The sea came and took everything. We're only an island now. Perhaps we'll be eaten by the sea next. The cliff did warn us, but people don't listen to nature like they used to. So poor nature howls in the void. To think that before the death of Nsanga-Norda, the cliff bellowed all through the night. But no one paid any attention.'

We looked in bewilderment at the great blue arm that swept the horizon over by Nsanga-Norda, and at the remains of the longest bridge in the world, still holding a pitiful skeleton of torn concrete suspended above the sea. None of us could believe our eyes. In the middle of the vast expanse of sea scattered with foam slept a huge arm of basalt, between thirty and fifty feet high, its head strangely resembling the Christ's head the Portuguese had taken from us.

'Heaven is returning it to us, but at what a price, my ancestors!' sighed the fat woman, who was still eating the mushrooms cooked in herbs.

'Heaven or the devil?' remarked the other old woman.

'When did the sea eat Nsanga-Norda?' asked the woman of the herbs.

'The day they killed Estina Bronzario. We were keeping the news from the world, because those fools on the Coast might have thought the sea was avenging them. In fact, Estina Bronzario's death was really a minor event.'

'Who killed Estina Bronzario, then?' asked Paolo Cerbante, who was tasting the water in which Nsanga-Norda was sleeping, to check if it was salty.

As for me, I was dumbstruck. I saw, or thought I saw, Estina Bronzario sitting on a large stone in the middle of the water, with her head in her hands. Standing behind her was Estina Benta, who was plaiting the wispy strands of her white hair.

'The sea will go back,' said a voice which sounded like that of the fat woman, who was eating seaweed, or perhaps it was Salmano Ruenta's.

'It'll go back,' burst out the man wearing the pectoral brooch. 'In the meantime, it's sleeping on a hundred thousand corpses, and the pipe-fish are gorging themselves.'

> The water has given
> The water can take back

119

It was when the land of the Albanicantes died
That the cliff gave birth to waters
All decked in salt and coral
It smelt of the time when everything was stone
And fire
The eye of the sage
Saw written on each grain of stone
This essential truth:
The water can take back what it has given
Then the fire will be born
To graze over the stone and the slate
The town will be so hungry because of its stupidity
So thirsty because of its shame
The cliff will want to sleep
And people will say: now is the end of time
What nonsense! Time has no end
For it was never created.

We sang the Coast version of the *Magnificat*, and all eyes filled with tears as we gazed at the unruffled sea and the play of its waves. On the horizon, a velvet-clad sky was bathed in air and mystery. It followed the watchful wheeling of the seagulls in the dense mist which was beginning to gather. I thought of Sarngata Nola who, with his heart full of bitterness, was still waiting for the day when Nsanga-Norda would kill ten thousand seven hundred and twelve perch-eaters. Our earthly lot is infinitely hard. The stones here have always known that. They've always shown us the shattered side of their dream. Like us, they were now trying to hide the death of Nsanga-Norda from the rest of the world. The surprising thing was that it lay just behind the impregnable cliff of Sarngata Nola's citadel, photographed a hundred thousand times a day.

6

Me

'I beg you, Gracia! I can't live without you. And I don't have the courage to die. Because I think no one has the right to die after Estina Bronzario. Let's go back to Valancia. We'll start our dream all over again. I don't know how to say this: my life comes from you and from you alone. It's from you that I've borrowed my soul. Be sensible, my love!'

'It's perfectly obvious, Paolo Cerbante, that it's because Helen is dead that your life now comes from me. You don't know me. You think I'm going to take on the shame the dead women have left me. Me, whose pride is lightning itself!'

'I'll die, then,' said Paolo Cerbante, twisting the black hair of his beard. 'I'll die because the emptiness around me is too stupid. It's true, I called this emptiness up myself. Without thinking, or perhaps out of curiosity, I don't know any more. In that non-sense that Valancia had become, even our love seemed like a corpse waiting for the police. You can't understand, and I wouldn't be so cruel as to ask you to do so. My dear love! What was there left in Valancia apart from Manuel Yeba's binges, and perhaps, too . . .?'

'And perhaps, too?'

'Sarngata Nola's thighs. I loved our love, and I had the greatest respect for it, the greatest veneration, too. But Estina Benta's desire threw itself at my throat every day and tried to strangle me. I sent her away. Because she belonged to our brother, Lorsa Lopez, who adored her, as we all knew. In any case, it was you I loved, not another woman. You alone. All of you. My body and my soul sang of you day and night. What do you expect! It's the depths of one's blood that are in control, man just obeys. Ah! If only you could . . . understand . . . and forgive. Forgive – that is, grow. Grow – that is, come once and for all into the world. I don't have the right any more to ask you

121

anything. Know at least that, for your sake, I sent Estina Benta to graze the pasture of her death. She told Lorsa Lopez that . . .'

'I'm not blaming you. You chose Helen. She was worth it. Her whole body was one terrible carnival. How could she inspire anything but unbridled passion? What else could she communicate but fire? She had a body that drew to it all dreams and all madness. She caught all the men of Valancia in the whirlwind of her charms. All of them! Philanderers, part-time womanisers, all the scatterers of semen. You queued up for her like spadefoot toads. She had a bite at you all.'

'You don't understand, Gracia!'

Here. I come to watch the sea from this rock. Paolo Cerbante's given up. He's left me here. Men are strange. He thinks I can . . . after Helen . . . No! I ask you! For me, the vagina is a temple. That's my choice. I could soil anything else, but not that, not my vagina. Down below, the stones murmur, no doubt laughing at Nsanga-Norda's misfortunes. The sky seems to be listening to them. The waves thread a hundred schemes that burst like soap bubbles. The earth has buried its heart for fear of cracking. When I turn round, I can see Paolo Cerbante. He's on top of the rock face that supports the remains of the bridge, suspended over the water. Night is falling. He calls out to me: 'Like Nsanga-Norda!'

Then he smiles a big smile, showing his white teeth in the dark. The stars come into the sky in laughing groups. The night descends deep into my being. Tomorrow, I'll go back to Valancia, since Nsanga-Norda no longer exists. There'll be those endless crowds of people coming to photograph the citadel. Perhaps I'll be able to forget the saliva that Paolo has spat into my heart. I'll be able to say shit to Estina Bronzario's memory. Shit, to that consummate hardness of hers . . . to the way she always saw the sun as mud, to her need to live her life bawling and shouting at the top of her voice. Shit! Shit! To her teeth of honour. To her tattoos. To her wayward memory. Shit to honour!

'Paolo Cerbante!'

He turns round. The same smile as before. And my heart aches. Perhaps we only come into this world to accept the unacceptable. Truth hates us. We have nothing in common with it. Yet, right in front of us, is the deep beauty of things. Even if that sea out there has eaten

Nsanga-Norda, it's no less beautiful in its robe of mystery studded with insects and night birds. Inhabited by the morbid roar of the waves. Why not die in this night? Join Nsanga-Norda. The sea! The way it has of taking the sky in its arms, and the deep limpidity of its promontories borne by the dazzling white chalk of its dream. And if each wave, each breath of wind were only praise offered up to God? All those perfumes. The chorus of insects backed by the heavy battery of the tree-frogs serenading the centenary of some conger eel.

'Tomorrow morning, I'll get up with my mind made up to go back to Valancia.'

The day we arrived, the militia gave us shelter in these two tents, one for the men and one for the women. We're eleven women. There are more men. Their tent is the same size as ours. I pack my things: my toothbrush, my towel, my make-up bag, my sheet. I wait for morning. In the dark, I watch the dark flow of the white-haired water that has eaten Nsanga-Norda. I'm not sleepy. I talk with my destiny and with the destiny of the devoured city. By now, the lotes must be watching over Paolo Cerbante's body. In this country, night has the appearance of divinity. It smells like infinity. Day here will never be more than a pathetic hole of blue, sickly light. Day here will always be as fordable as the Rouvièra Verda upriver from the bayou. Only the night has things to say to the soul. Only it can unite our bodies with the vast truculence of the universe.

> *I keep you in the immortal*
> *Memory of my aberrant vagina*
> *I lay upon you my breast*
> *And my flagellated flanks*
> *And that green soul*
> *That rises*
> *To meet a pagan heart.*
> *I lay upon you the choice*
> *Of my foolish loins.*
> *How I wish*
> *You had been made of straw*
> *And nitrogen too perhaps*
> *Free to roam the seas . . .*

I sing the joy of my solitude bristling with pride. Like fetishes spiked with nails. I nurse it like a beloved child. This world is an immense corpse fighting to live by every means. A battle of stones. A battle of nitrogen. A battle of blood. A battle engaged between the silence of the Island of Solitudes and the din of the Atlantic. A battle between the rapt silence of the sandstone loaves and the spyglass of the stars. Already, I can hear Lorsa Lopez's barking: Valancia is very near. Very near, too, Nansa Mopata's well-tuned laugh. I see the Rouvièra Verda taking its water dues down to the Atlantic. I see the coppery buttresses of the citadel shattering the horizon into a thousand pieces.

Lorsa Lopez

Great crowds stream across the bayou at the place where Fr Bona of the Sacristy crossed on the day of the crime. We can't understand it: men, women and children; Mahometans, Christians, Hindus and homodeists; Orientals dressed in all the colours of the rainbow and wearing extravagant hats – all of them mounting their assault on the hill to photograph Sarngata Nola's stone monster. The sea has spewed them up like termites. The arrogant, incestuous construction, nesting place of eagles and vultures, turns its leaden back on the nine o'clock sun. The shapes and the barbaric glitter of the walls, weather-beaten by rain and wind, dance in the glare. Always and everywhere, man has played at laying stones on top of stones, to hide the wound of his fragility. I look at the crushing smile of the citadel seated on its cliff-top plinth. I liken those laughing stones to the taciturn spirit of the water which drank and dismembered Nsanga-Norda, and swallowed the once longest bridge in the world. The khaki water innocently weaving its fleece of foam around the Island of Solitudes. The water gorged with arches, menhirs, minarets with their hard iron bones, triumphal arches, corbels and the never-ending ventriloquism of the muezzins. The water on to which, this evening, the Southern Cross will throw its dismayed gaze, while in its belly lotes and piranhas swarm like crabs, dancing the unending rumpus of that other dimension of things. We are the wounded, wrenched from the sky, the water and the hard, grey-thinking stones.

'I'm leaving,' Fartamio Andra do Nguélo Ndalo said to her sister, Fartamio Andra. 'People without head or tail are beginning to come here. And as for that one, I ask you! You can hear him coming from a long way off because he stinks like a pleistocene rat. He must have cadged that cadaver's walk of his from the devil.'

'He's the new muezzin,' explained Anna Maria.

'Only one thing still works in this town: death,' said Fartamio Andra do Nguélo Ndalo.

Fartamio Andra do Nguélo Ndalo thought she was going to give up the ghost the day Espanzo Lambert arrived.

'As long as you live,' she said to Fartamio Andra, 'make sure the Coast remains the Coast. Estina Bronzario's Coast, I mean. Take care that it doesn't become the Nsanga-Nordans' public toilet.'

We thought she was going to give up her soul around four o'clock. Members of the Founders Line don't die unexpectedly. They always know the time of their death. Fartamio Andra Louta, Fartamio Andra do Nguélo Ndalo's grandmother, knew the day and the hour of her death three weeks in advance. 'I shall die on the day the Mahometans gorge themselves, at the hour of the leopard.'

Fartamio Andra do Nguélo Ndalo asked for her Nsanga-Norda secretary-bird broth to be prepared, always the last meal of members of the Line.

'Don't put too much salt in it. In fact, I'd rather you didn't put any in at all. Salt isn't good for the journey of death.'

She'd no sooner eaten it than she brought it all up again. Her temperature was rising very fast. Manuel Yeba decided to put his medical knowledge to use. He listened with his dinaural stethoscope and had difficulty disguising his uneasiness. The apparatus was in any case very old. We knew that he was exercising his previous day's binge rather than his profession. And we all smiled when he diagnosed the 'blue heart', or Valtano sickness. We knew that no one had suffered from that sickness since the first decapitalisation war. The sickness had killed three hundred people in Valtano in two weeks. Then Marcio Louta had found the bronze-juice cure. The sickness departed and that was the end of it. Manuel Yeba prescribed a half a glass of bronze-juice morning, noon and evening.

'You drink too much, doctor,' said Fartamio Andra, who was wondering what Manuel intended doing with the optical diaphragm and the magnifying glass he was fiddling with like a little boy.

'You're too old to understand medicine,' said Manuel Yeba.

He asked Anna Maria to check if there was enough agave oil in the house for the washing of the corpse.

126

'She's of the Line. You can't send her off with agave oil. She must have bronze-water and essences of *sesban*.'

'Send discreetly for the priest.'

'She'll think we're preparing for her death,' Fartamio Andra objected. 'We mustn't upset her like that.'

We kept our eyes on her chest, watching for the moment when the cold would set in. In spite of his hangover, Manuel Yeba's sorrow was clearly real. He was afraid she would die in his arms, so he went outside, pretending he was going to fetch the compass.

'What's the compass for?' asked Anna Maria, in surprise.

'The Nsanga-Norda compass: to help the heart on its journey.'

The sick woman was gasping, rather than breathing. Her mouth and nostrils filled continuously with a white, gluey substance that stank of putrefaction.

'Make sure Valancia stays Valancia,' said the dying woman.

At that moment, Espanzo Lambert came in, his head perched on top of his seven feet four-and-a-half inches, which always made people laugh because of the infinite smallness of his bald head framed by the most frightful ears. He was a poor copy of Carlanzo Mana of the ministry, and as stupid as he had been.

'Is she dead?' asked Espanzo Lambert, anointed with his profound stupidity and the fetid smell of a gout-ridden hypochondriac with hypgoma on his last legs.

No one answered him. Then Manuel Yeba arrived, and once more set about deploying his medical knowledge, drowned as it was in the after-effects of his binge. He listened with the stethoscope as one listens to a bad piece of music. What use could he be? His professional training had long since been flung on to the ceiling of his brain, where it clung until the occasional desperate case obliged him to retrieve it. He began to hunt feverishly for something in his big elephant-hide briefcase, which contained his dilapidated equipment and the manuscript copy of his diploma, signed by the celebrated professor of general medicine, Landro Lopez Mouramorio.

The priest swept in. The muezzin suggested they go and look at the garden, so as to keep him away from the poor woman, who was preparing for death with such great dignity.

'But there's no time to lose,' the priest told the muezzin.

He entered the room with his implements: stoup, monstrance, prayer book and crucifix. The dying woman smiled a big limpid smile on seeing the priest.

'How are you, Fr Roguerio?'

'How are you, Madame Bronzario?'

The priest had never managed to call people by their correct names. He always called Manuel Yeba 'Comrade Ruenta', even though Manuel Yeba himself never tired reminding him that Salmano Ruenta had been murdered and that he must now be sleeping sweetly in the arms of Comrade Abraham, between Lazarus and Kisito.

'But Salmano took communion yesterday at the six o'clock mass. I asked him to bring me three kilos of potatoes on Sunday.'

'No, Father. He was killed sixteen years ago and his bones are waiting for the police on the Nsanga-Norda road.'

'How are you, Father?' the sick woman asked again.

'I'm well, Madame Bronzario.'

'And your haemorrhoids?'

This was followed by a long silence. Even Fartamio Andra, who was an expert at breaking silences, didn't quite know how to set about restarting the conversation this time. The sick woman's body was slowly being born into the final silence. In a sudden burst of lucidity, she announced that she wanted to die in the presence of Fartamio Andra alone.

'It'll be more peaceful that way. She'll close my mouth and my eyes.'

We were preparing to leave when Espanzo Lambert gave a small irritated laugh.

'No, Madame Andra do Nguélo Ndalo, you can't die just yet. You must wait for the police. They won't be long now.'

The dying woman emerged from her coma as you emerge from sleep after your wedding night. She looked at Espanzo Lambert. Her eyes were inhabited by a strange glow. She looked to see if Fartamio Andra and Manuel Yeba were there.

'We're with you,' said Manuel Yeba.

At that moment Lorsa Lopez arrived, dressed in a billowing garment made of grass, which he'd woven with his own hands and painted with kaolin. Lorsa Lopez was back from the Island of Solitudes. His beard and hair fell around him. He drew up a chair and on it placed his right foot, covered with mud, that same mud that Sarngata Nola had left on the tiles the day he'd come to insult Estina Bronzario. He asked for a cup of citronella, which Anna Maria prepared for him. When he'd drunk it, he took the female hand of the dying woman, and began to play with it. He kissed it three times and said: 'You can die, sister. The police won't be coming, for Nsanga-Norda is now sleeping under seven hundred and fifteen feet of salt and water.'

He nibbled a stale crust of kola. Then he began to tell us his own version of his crime.

'We're a people of honour. And honour means choice. The seven tattoos that we have on our hearts signify choice. We of the Coast aren't made to muddle along in any kind of existence. Now that Nsanga-Norda hasn't had time to send its police, I'll have to wait for the Good Lord to judge my crime. Do you understand? I loved her madly. At the slightest fear I went and buried myself in the depths of her body. I dug my soul into the volcano of her desire. I should have killed myself, but death is too trivial for a monster like me. You understand, sisters! It's better that way. Since the police haven't come, I alone in the world know why I killed her. I and the stars. I and the stones of the bayou. I and God. Say, sisters, you wouldn't have a drop of bronze-water? I'm thirsty. What do you expect! After all, this crime wasn't mine alone!'

We were all listening to Lorsa Lopez talking about the Island of Solitudes and no one saw Fartamio Andra do Nguélo Ndalo die. She must have died like a shadow to avoid disturbing us.